Rais

Raised as a Goon 5

1

Lock Down Publications and Ca$h
Presents
Raised as a Goon 5
A Novel by *Ghost*

Lock Down Publications

P.O. Box 870494

Mesquite, Tx 75187

First Edition August 2018

Printed in the United States of America

Lock Down Publications

Like our page on Facebook: Lock Down Publications @

www.facebook.com/lockdownpublications.ldp

Cover design and layout by: **Dynasty CoverMe**

Book interior design by: **Shawn Walker**

Editor: **Sunny Giovanni**

Ghost

Stay Connected with Us!

Text **LOCKDOWN** to 22828 to stay up-to-date with new releases, sneak peaks, contests and more…

Thank you!

Ghost

Submission Guidelines:

Submit the first three chapters of your completed manuscript to ldpsubmissions@gmail.com,
Subject line: Your book's title.
The manuscript must be in a .doc file and sent as an attachment. Document should be in Times New Roman, double spaced and in size 12 font. Also, provide your synopsis and full contact information. If sending multiple submissions, they must each be in a separate email.

Have a story but no way to send it electronically? You can still submit to LDP/Ca$h Presents. Send in the first three chapters, written or typed, of your completed manuscript to:

LDP: Submissions Dept
Po Box 870494
Mesquite, Tx 75187

DO NOT send original manuscript. Must be a duplicate.

Provide your synopsis and a cover letter containing your full contact information.

Thanks for considering LDP and Ca$h Presents.

Ghost

Raised as a Goon 5

DEDICATION

This book is dedicated to my precious, beautiful Baby Girl, the love of my life, 3/10.

ACKNOWLEDGEMENTS

I would like the thank the Boss Man and C.E.O of LDP, Cash. Thank you for this opportunity. Your wisdom, motivation and encouragement are appreciated. Thanks, Bruh.

To the Queen and C.O.O of LDP, thank you for all that you do Sis. Your hard work, dedication and loyalty to this company never goes unnoticed.

The grind is real. The loyalty in this family is real. I'm riding with LDP 'til the wheels fall off. The GAME IS OURS!

Message To The Readers:

I sincerely appreciate ya'll rocking with me throughout this entire series. Thank you for allowing me to share my story.

Chapter 1

Taurus

"Taurus! Taurus! Oh my God! She killed that girl! She killed that girl!" My mother fell to the ground on both of her knees. She hopped up and ran into my arms, crying against my chest, her breath hard with every rise and fall of her chest. Her eyes were bloodshot and puffy as if she'd been crying all day. Before I could ask her what it was that she was talking about, her body went limp against me.

I leaned over and struggled to get her back to her feet. "Mama, what are you talking about? Who killed what girl?" I asked, looking into her red face.

Mascara mixed with tears, dripped from her chin and onto her sundress. The wind blew lightly, causing her curly hair to blow into her face. It was hot and humid. The sun heated up the back of my neck and forehead. Sweat slid down the side of my face. I felt the beats of my heart speed up as I anticipated the worst of the worst news from her.

She got to her feet and shook her head, trying to tell me something but only managed a whimper before tears sailed down her cheeks worst then before. She pointed toward the house and took off running toward it with me on her heels.

I rushed up Blaze's porch steps and bumped the front door wide open. The doorknob slammed into the wall and created a big hole. Drywall fell out of the hole and dropped to the Welcome mat. I got into the living room and looked around in a panic. My mother fell to her knees once again and began to break down. She put her forehead on the floor and sobbed at the top of her lungs. As much as I wanted to comfort her, I knew I had to get to the bottom of what was going on. I rubbed her back and made my way through the house, listening intently.

"Princess! Baby, where are you? Blaze? Where are y'all at?" I jogged through the house until I got to the middle of it, right by the staircase that led upstairs to the second level.

I looked up the flight of stairs with my throat drier than I ever remembered it being before. I was afraid of what I was about to encounter. There had been so many things that had taken place within the last month. Things that told me that I needed to get the hell out of the United States or else my family, as well as myself, were going to pay the consequences.

I swallowed and made my way up the upstairs. When I got to the top I could hear my daughter Jahliya screaming at the top of her lungs. She was usually a very quiet child. For her to be making so much noise, something had to be utterly wrong. I jogged down the hallway toward her, pushing in one door after the next. I found her on the other side of the third door I'd pushed in, sitting in the middle of the bed, with big throw pillows all around her. I guessed it was to prevent her from falling off of the bed.

When she saw me, she began to bounce up and down, screaming with her arms outstretched, signaling for me to pick her up.

I rushed to the bed, knocked two pillows out of the way, scooped her into the air and hugged her. "Calm down, Lil' mama. It's okay. Daddy right here.

I got you, baby." I kissed her cheek and continued to bounce her while I patted her on her pull-up.

Very slowly she began to calm herself. She coughed a couple times, then laid her face into the crux of my neck.

I stepped out of the bedroom with her and made my way back down the long hallway, opening doors as I went. Finally, I made it to Blaze's master bedroom and attempted to twist the knob, finding it locked. I frowned and pounded on the door. "Blaze! Princess! Open this damn door!" I pounded more furiously.

This sent Jahliya over the edge. She began to scream, jumping up and down in my arms. I wouldn't find out until later that she was suffering from an ear infection that she'd had for two days.

My mother appeared at the end of the hall, wiping at her face with a Kleenex. It felt as if it were ten degrees hotter than it had been on the first level of Blaze's crib. I could feel the sweat pouring down my back. "Give her to me, Taurus. She doesn't need to see what you're about to see. Here." She held out her hands for Jahliya, walking toward us.

Jahliya must've known what was about to take place because she started to jump up and down in my arms wildly, shaking her head. "No! Grandma! No!" She hollered.

I handed her to my mother with Jahliya pulling on my shirt. She broke into a fit. Her little face turned beet red. My mother took her down the stairs. I could hear her calling for me the entire time.

I tried the lock to the bedroom door again, jiggling it hard. "Open this fucking door!" I took a step back, mugged it, expecting for it to be opened in any second. When nothing happened, I took two steps back and rushed it shoulder first. Crashing into it, the door splintered but didn't open. "Open this door!" I backed up five paces, then ran at it again with my shoulder. This time so hard that it fell inward.

The knob dropped to the floor. The door was partway off the hinges. Wood splinters decorated the carpet below it. There, in the middle of the carpet, was a pregnant Blaze on her knees giving CPR to Princess. She pinched her nose and blew into her mouth. She clasped her fists together and pressed on her chest over and over again with tears in her eyes. Beside Princess' body was an all-white extension cord.

"I'm sorry, Taurus. I didn't mean to do it. I didn't mean to, I swear." She cried, continuing to give her CPR.

I felt like my heart had stopped as I looked down and at the body of Princess. She was dress in a pair of Capris. No shirt, just a bra, and bare feet. Her eyes were closed tightly. She looked as if she were in intense pain. Her face was dark brown, almost blue. She had red lines around her neck, I was guessing from where Blaze had choked her out with the white extension cord.

I dropped to my knees and crawled across the floor toward her. "Blaze, what the fuck did you do? What the fuck did you do to my baby?" I hollered, nudging her out of the way and taking over the duties of CPR. I pressed Princess' chest, then pinched her nose and blew into her mouth over and over.

Blaze backed all the way up to her dresser with her knees to her chest. Tears streamed down her face. She covered her face with her hands and cried into them. "I'm sorry, Taurus. She came at me. She tried to fuck me up. You should see these knots on the back of my head. I'm so, so sorry."

I continued my chest compressions and blowing into her mouth. "Come on, Princess. Come on, baby. Come on. You're stronger than this. Come back to me. I need you, boo. Daddy needs you to fight." I pinched her nose once again and blew into her mouth. Her chest rose and then fell. I laid my head on her chest, listening for a heartbeat and detecting none. I felt like I was about to lose my mind.

Blaze crawled over to me and pulled my shirt. "Taurus! Please forgive me, baby. I swear I was defending myself. I would have never gone at her. She came at me. You gotta believe me." She cried with snot dripping out of her nose.

I brushed her hand off of me. "Get the fuck away from me, Blaze. You killed my baby. You took her life!" I mugged her and had visions of choking her out; bodying her and laying her right beside Princess. I couldn't believe what she'd done. She'd hurt the only woman I had ever loved with all of my heart. My seven. My completion. The female version of me. I felt like stomping a mudhole into Blaze with no mercy.

My mother came part way into the room. She saw what was going on and fell to her knees again. "Is she dead? Taurus, please tell me that girl ain't dead!" She screamed, got up and ran down the hallway. "I'm calling the Paramedics."

Blaze kneeled with her hands covering her face. "I'm sorry, Taurus. What do you want me to do? I'll do anything, I swear." She crawled back over to me and tried to lay her head on my shoulder. The bulge in her middle was evident.

I jerked my shoulder away from her, pushed her backward, took the .9 millimeter off my waist and extended my arm, aiming it at her, cocking the hammer. "Bitch, I should blow yo' muthafucking head off." Tears threatened to escape me. A dry lump formed in my throat, making it hard for me to swallow.

Blaze looked into my eyes and squeezed her lids together. More tears slid down her face before she opened them again. She sniffed loudly and nodded, holding her hand out in the shape of a lowercase T. "Just do it, Taurus. I don't even care no more. Shoot me. Take me away from this bullshit because I can't go to prison. I'd rather die first." She whimpered. She crawled across the carpet until her forehead was an inch away from the barrel of my pistol. She pulled it so that it was up against her skin.

I bit into my lower lip and put my finger on the trigger, ready to blow her brains out, when she lowered one of her hands and placed it up under her stomach. It reminded me that she was carrying our unborn child. I was so glad that she had because I was seconds away from splattering her all over the carpet. I scrunched my face and shook my head. "Just get the fuck away from me right now, Blaze. Go downstairs before I body yo' ass!" I pointed with the gun toward the open door.

She got to her feet and looked down on me as I began my chest compressions again. "This ain't my fault, Taurus. I didn't want this to happen. I was more than cool with staying in my own lane. She came at me. What was I supposed to do?" She backed into the bathroom that was located to the right of her bed and slammed the door.

As soon as it closed, all the floodgates were opened in me. Tears got to pouring out of my eyes as I looked down at the lifeless Princess. All of the memories that we'd shared went through my mind. Each one causing me to become sicker than the one before it. A person never knew how much they loved another until they were gone. At that moment, I realized how much I loved Princess with all my soul. I didn't know what I would do without her being on this earth.

My mother appeared in the doorway with the paramedics in what seemed like seconds later. They rushed in, and I stood up while they went to work on Princess. One of them pulled out a defibrillator, placing it on her chest. As soon as it was activated, he yelled clear. She jerked off of the floor. He repeated the process while I wiped the tears out of my eyes. Two more paramedics came in. They kneeled and huddled around her, all using their expertise. I felt like I couldn't breathe or think straight. I prayed to the Lord above for Him to spare her life. I asked him to take mine instead. To make me her sacrifice. I was willing to pay any penalty just as long as Princess received breath in her lungs again.

Blaze came out of the bathroom and walked past the group of working paramedics.

I waited until she got into the hallway and slipped behind her, grabbing her arm. "Where the fuck you think you finna, go?" I asked, turning her around to face me.

She swallowed and looked over my shoulder. "Aw, so that's how you finna do it? You finna have these people lock me up?" She wiped a tear from her cheek and looked up to me.

Two more paramedics climbed the stairs with a stretcher in their hands. They ran past us and into Blaze's bedroom. They set it beside Princess and started to load her on to it. I didn't know what was going on. I prayed that it meant good news.

Blaze turned her back to me and jogged toward the stairs. She stopped when she got to the top of them and looked down them with her eyes wide open. "Shit." She faced me. "What y'all gon' tell them police, Taurus? I swear to God I didn't mean for this to happen." She whispered, looking back down the stairs.

"Excuse us. Out of the way. We're in a hurry!" One of the Paramedics hollered.

He and a group of his coworkers stormed past with Princess on the stretcher. She had an oxygen mask over her face and IVs in her arms. They carried her down the stairs and out of the house. I followed close behind. My mother was in the living room talking to two police officers.

"Hey, where are y'all taking her?" I yelled.

"Mount Sinai off of University Avenue!" Hollered the driver of the ambulance.

Blaze stormed out of the house and jumped into her pink Lexus.

Before she could get out of the driveway, I threw open the door and jumped in beside her. "Where the fuck is you going, Blaze?"

She started the ignition and put her car into reverse. "I can't go to jail for this shit, Taurus. I'm not about to have my baby in nobody's jail cell. Screw that." She stepped on the gas and nearly backed into one of the paramedics. He jumped out of the way just in time, throwing his arms into the air in anger. Blaze acted as if she didn't see him. She put the car into first gear and pulled away from the big house, flying down the street like a bat out of hell.

I mugged the side of her head. I was fuming. So mad that my palms were sweating. I wanted to do something to her to cause her pain. Wished that she weren't pregnant with my seed. Had she not been, I would have killed her back when we were upstairs in her room. "Blaze, tell me what happened. How did you wind up doing what you did to her?"

She made a right onto a busy intersection. We rode on it for a moment before jumping on the highway. She shook her head and sighed. "I was in the living room, minding my business. Your mother had just taken Jahliya out of the tub. She was going to make her something to eat, so she handed her to me. Princess had taken a walk around the block or somethin', I don't know. All I do know is that when she came back she saw me holding you guys' daughter and flipped her lid. She yanked Jahliya out of my arms, took her upstairs, and came back down and got into my face. You already know how she is."

She sped past a pick-up truck that had a gang of smoke coming from the muffler. She rolled up her window and turned the air conditioner on blast, fixing the vent so that it blew on her.

"And, what else happened?" I was getting angry again.

"Well, she started calling me out of my name, saying that I was a homewrecker, and saying that she should kick our baby out of me. That she wasn't so sure that it was yours anyway. That I was a dirty, lowlife stripper looking to capitalize off of you and y'alls family. Had the nerve to slap me across the face and knock me to the couch. After I fell, she jumped on my back and punched me in the head about fifty times until I got dizzy and passed out."

Just hearing what she'd said so far was making me miss Princess even more. I had to find a way to get her to drive to Mount Sinai Hospital, so I could find out if she was okay. I didn't think that they'd put a breathing mask on her if they didn't need to. I'd been around enough murders to know that when you're gone after they're done doing what they're going to do, they put you in a body bag and that's just that.

"When I came to, she was upstairs going on a rampage, snapping about you choosing me over her. How you've hurt her heart, and how she was going to kill me. Your mother was trying to tell her to let it go. But you already know how hardheaded Princess is. I guess her mind was made up. To make this long story short, I took the cord that the lamps were hooked up to in the living room, crept up behind her ass while she was changing Jahliya's pamper, wrapped it around her neck, and fell to the floor with her right on my bedroom floor. Your mother rushed in and grabbed Jahliya. Princess struggled against me, but I wasn't letting her ass go. I felt like if I had she would have gotten one of your guns and killed me. After a while she stopped struggling, and by that time I'd come to the realization that I might have killed her. I stood up, and she was laid out flat on her back. Your mother saw it from a distance. She ran toward the bedroom and I slammed the door in her face. A few minutes later, I'm guessing you pulled up." She looked over to me. "I didn't know what else to do, Taurus. You know that girl would have killed me first. You can't just think about what I did to her without flipping the script. I'm pregnant, and I have to protect our child as well as myself. This is bigger than just her. You have to see that." She sniffed and swallowed.

I didn't know what to say in that moment. I guess on one hand she was right. Princess was a savage just like me. She'd repeated time and time again that she was going to kill Blaze one day. As much as I believed her, I'd never taken the proper precaution to prevent it. I just figured that in time they would learn to get along with each other. After all, they would both have my children. I felt responsible for their relationship. But I also felt like it had been pointless to cry over spilled milk. Both knew what it was before they got deeply involved with me. I was just wishing I'd kept them separated.

"Blaze, I don't even know what to say right now. I got a whole lot of thinking to do. What I want to know right now is where do you think you're going?"

She shrugged. "I don't know, Taurus. I just had to get out of there. I can't go to jail if that girl dies. You know I wouldn't make it in there." She whimpered.

"She ain't finna die! Stop saying that shit. She way too strong for that." I snapped. "You ain't going to no jail, and you ain't about to run nowhere. Take this car to Mount Sinai so I can make sure she's good. After we confirm that, you and I are going to get an understanding. No matter what, you about to have my shorty, so I gotta keep you close. Y'all gotta stop all this fucking fighting. We're too grown for this shit. Get in that lane and head toward University Avenue."

She followed my directives and shook her head. "Taurus, what am I gon' do if they find out that I'm the one that did this to her? When I left your mother was talking to two detectives."

I shook my head. "They weren't detectives, they were only regular police. My mother would never tell them what really happened. She seasoned better than that. She'll come up with something. Whatever that is, we gon' have to stick to that script. I'm sure that as soon as they leave her she gon' hit my phone. This ain't her first rodeo." I was confident that my mother would spin the law and hold Blaze down even if she didn't want to. Our family didn't fuck with the police on no level. We took the law into our own hands. Always had.

Blaze nodded and exhaled loudly. "Okay, Taurus. I know you love her way more than you do me, but please don't let them take me away. I would never do that to you."

Chapter 2

My mother did just like I thought she would. She told the police that Princess had been struggling with depression, and on that particular day she'd tried to hang herself. My mother said that she'd bussed through the bedroom door and found her hanging from the shower pole in the bathroom, took her down and performed CPR on her before contacting the paramedics. When they'd asked who else had been in the home she told them no one. That Blaze and I had come seconds before the ambulance arrived. That Blaze had been so distraught she was unable to take the sights of the scene. She'd run off and I was in pursuit of her. She was sure that they'd bought the story but had questions about the extension cord that Blaze had used. It was missing from the scene, taken by Blaze. She'd thrown it into the river.

The medical staff were able to save Princess. She stayed in the hospital for a full two weeks after she came to. Then they sent her directly from there to a psychiatric hospital to be evaluated for seventy-two hours. I visited her on the second day. She was already up and seemed to be at full strength.

I couldn't believe it. They allowed for us to visit in a small room. It had two cushion-covered stools and a metal table. The walls were white bricked. On the ceiling hung a long light that made the room super bright. I squinted the entire visit and tried to avoid a serious migraine. I'd been sitting for twenty minutes when they brought Princess. The orderly opened the door, walked her inside and made sure that she was seated before he backed out of the room with a stern look on his face.

He was heavy-set with a rosy face, balding in the middle of his head and smelled of sweat. "You have forty-five minutes. If there is an issue, push the red button on the side of the table. We'll be in here in no time." He looked down at Princess while saying this before held left the room.

Princess waited until the door closed before she jumped up, ran around the table and smacked me so hard that I fell off of the stool onto my right hand. "You let this punk bitch live after what she's done to me? What the fuck is wrong with you?" She yelled with tears in her eyes.

I hopped up and snatched her up, slamming her against the wall, picking her up so that her feet were dangling in the air. She wore a cloth white gown. It was so thin that I could make out her nudity underneath it. "What the fuck is wrong with you?"

She twisted wildly and kicked at me. "Let me go, Taurus! Put me down and go snatch that bitch up!" She peeled my fingers from her gown and dropped to her feet.

"She said you beat the shit out of her first. Then you were talking about how you were going to kill her. What was she supposed to do, Princess? Huh?"

She bucked her eyes and jerked her head backward. "Aw, so now you even defending this bitch over me!" She scrunched her face and threw her guards into the air. "You finna have to whoop my ass, Taurus. I'm serious. That bitch damn near killed me, and you're defending her. Fuck this shit." She rushed me, swinging her fists wildly. Her eyes were lowered into slits. Her face balled into a menacing scowl. Tears dripped off of her chin.

She swung two blows as hard as she could. I blocked them with my forearm and grabbed her by the neck. I held her against the wall once again, applying pressure. When it came to Princess, she ain't understand nothing but that rough and tough shit. I couldn't treat her like the average female because deep down she had the heart of a pure goon. She slapped at my arms.

I leaned into her face and smashed my forehead against hers. "Princess, stop playing these games with me. You already know I ain't about to let you put yo' fucking hands on me. Now I ain't picking nobody's side. Both of y'all need to grow the fuck up and be women. Its kids involved."

Princess clenched her jaw and curled her upper lip, looking into my eyes. "Nigga, if you don't take yo' muthafucking hands from around my neck, I swear to God whenever you do, one of us gon' have to die. Get yo' fucking hands off of me, Taurus. Now!" She slapped at my hand around her neck, tilted her head and bit into it like a Pitbull.

I jerked my hand away and balled up my fist, seconds away from bussing her in the mouth. I'd never gone that far with her before, but she was pressing her luck.

She turned her back to me and shook her head, looking over her shoulder at me. "She wasn't ever supposed to have your child in her body, Taurus. That bitch bussed a move on you, and you let it happen. It's the oldest fucking trick in the book. Now I'm supposed to accept it?" She lowered her head and sat on the stool. "You know I can't accept what she did to me, right? You sit up here hollering that there are children involved and all that shit. I get that, but I can't accept this. That bitch could have killed me." She balled her hands into fists and stood up, shaking her head, squeezing her eyelids tightly and biting on her bottom lip.

I stood in front of her and took a hold of her wrists. Pulled her to me and wrapped my arms around her. "Baby girl, we'll figure this thing out. You already know that ain't nobody about to hurt you and get away with it. We just gotta be smart right now." I kissed her on the forehead, letting out a deep sigh. My mind was all over the place.

"Taurus, you know that ain't how we get down though. If it was anybody else, you would have already handled your business. Nigga, you killed your own brother for some of the things that he did to me. Now, just because you got a thing for this bitch we're waiting to make her pay for what she did to me. It's bigger than what's in her stomach. I know you care about her, don't you?" She broke our embrace and took a step back, looking up at me with menacing eyes.

I tried my best to avoid making eye contact with her. I never liked lying to Princess and hadn't ever since we'd been together. There was no way that I could tell her that I cared about Blaze. Not after what she'd done to her. But the reality was that I'd had strong feelings for Blaze since before me and Princess had ever met. She'd been my escape from the slums. My oasis. She'd shown me a different world outside of the ghetto. It was because of her that

I was able to think bigger than just the hood. I cared about her a lot. I didn't think about her nearly as much as I did about Princess, but in all honesty, it was close. Blaze had been one hunnit since day one, and always tried to find ways and avenues to help me advance in the game. I remembered her telling me that she felt I was supposed to be a rich nigga. That she was going to make sure that when it was all said and done that I would be. Thus far, she'd stuck to her word because my chips were all the way up.

Princess pushed me in the chest with both hands. "Get the fuck away from me, Taurus. Damn." She shook her head and turned her back to me again. "We've been through all of this bullshit together, and in the end, this is what it boils down to? Blaze?" She looked into the distance, dumbfounded. She sucked her teeth and faced me again. "What is it about this bitch, because I don't get it? Don't bring up the fact that she's pregnant either, because I'm not stupid; it's bigger than that." She walked into my face. "Do you wanna be with her over me, Taurus? Be honest."

I exhaled loudly and looked into her brown eyes, frustrated. "Baby, I ain't thinking about being with nobody on that level right now. I gotta get y'all the fuck out of this country. It's so much shit going on with me and Hood Rich that it ain't safe here no more. I don't know when our enemies gon' strike. Before they do, I gotta make sure my women are safe and sound."

Princess looked up at me with a slight smile on her face. "Your women, huh? Oh, so you just think that everybody belongs to you. We're all your women. Everybody gon' fawn all over Taurus for the rest of our lives. You'll never have to make a decision, right?" She stepped closer to my face.

I had my head tilted toward the ceiling, trying to calm down. Not only was she getting on my nerves with being all up in my face, but her words held so much truth and the truth always stung like a muthafucka.

I didn't feel like I needed to decide between her and Blaze no time soon. I felt like there were more important things on my plate that I had to take care of first. Who I was looking to settle down with was at the very bottom of my list. I nudged her just enough to move her out of my face.

Princess was little— about 5'4" and 115 pounds. The most I'd ever seen her get up to was about 120. I was a rock-solid 6'2", 200 pounds; real muscular. So even when I did my best to barely nudge her, she wound up stumbling backward a few feet.

She bucked her eyes then closed them tight as tears spilled from them. "Taurus, I love you. You know I do. I'll never let this bitch take you away from me." She started to walk toward me again.

"Princess, you are overthinking shit again. You already know it's me and you forever. Ain't nothing finna change that. Not Blaze, not our circumstances. Not her having my child. None of that. I love you. Always have and always will. Damn."

"More than her? That's all I wanna know. Do you love me more than that bitch? Keep it real." She looked up and into my eyes, searching them for the truth. She grabbed a hold of my shirt and balled it into her fist.

"Without a shadow of a doubt. I don't love anyone on this earth as much as I love you. It's us against the world." I grabbed a handful of her hair that was flowing down her back and yanked her head backward. Kissed along her neck where the ligature marks had been from the extension cord. Licked all over them, then sucked with my lips.

She winced and moaned deep within her throat. Then, she reached in between us and unbuttoned my pants, sticking her hand inside of my Polo boxers while I sucked and kissed all over her juicy lips. "Mmm, Taurus. I'm not stupid, and I'm not letting this shit go. We gotta talk about this some more when I get out of here, but for now, we got like fifteen minutes. I need some of my daddy real quick." She licked my lips, sucking them into her mouth.

I yanked her gown around her waist and picked her lil' ass up into the air. She wrapped her legs around me and reached under her ass to line me up so I could enter that pussy. I could feel my head on her sex lips, throbbing, ready to feel her.

"I'm finna kill this pussy, baby girl. Daddy finna murder this shit."

She bit into my neck. I could feel her teeth breaking the skin. A chill went down my spine. My breathing got heavy. I slammed her down onto my pipe and bent my knees just enough to give me leverage. I gripped her fat ass booty, bouncing her, making her take the whole pipe while she dug her nails into my shoulder blades.

"Uh! Fuck! Shit, Taurus! Fuck me! Fuck me! Fuck me! I'm. Your. Baby. Girl. Shit! Daddy!" She tightened her legs around my lower back and sucked on my ear, sticking her tongue inside of it.

I bounced her with my eyes closed. Princess always had a tight, wet pussy that leaked every time my dick went in and out of it. It felt like a wet fist milking me. "This my pussy. This. Pussy. Belong. To. Daddy!" I slammed her down again and again.

She whimpered in my ear, breathing heavily, with her mouth agape. Her tongue trailed all over her thick lips.

I laid her on to the metal table, pushed her knees to her chest, and got to long-stroking her. I watched my dick open her wide while it ran in and out of her box. It was coated in her cream. The gown had risen above her titties. She pulled on the nipples. They were erect and stood out from her mound about an inch. I loved watching her play with them as the scent of her pussy wafted up to my nose, intoxicating me.

"Taurus! Taurus! Uhh-fuck! Taurus! Yes. Daddy! Yes! Fuck me, Daddy! Fuck yo' Princess!" She threw her head back and groaned loudly before cumming all over my dick. Her pussy's walls pulsated around my stalk, squeezing it for dear life.

I kept right on stabbing with a vengeance, hitting that pussy as hard as I could while sucking on her neck. She dug her nails into my lower back and humped into me several times as hard as she could. It was just enough to send me over the edge. I sped up the pace and popped my back, digging deeper and deeper until my body tensed up, and I felt my climax coming from all over me. "Uh. Uh. Shit, Princess. Shit. You my baby! You belong to me!" I hollered, cumming deep within her belly, long-stroking her and spitting globs of myself into her.

When we finally climbed off of the table, I sat on the stool and she straddled me. She laid her head on my shoulder and rubbed the side of my face. I could smell her pussy in the air and it was causing me to become hard all over again.

She rubbed her cheek against mine and kissed my lips, positioning herself so that she could feel my pipe better. "Baby, we've been through way too much together for me to just let anybody steal you away. I ain't going. You keep saying that I'm overreacting, but I know you care about that girl, Taurus. I saw that look in your eyes the first time I ever saw you and Blaze in the same room together." She continued to rub my face. "Taurus, I can't function as long as I know that bitch is alive. I can't accept what she did to me, or the feelings you have for her. I gotta body this bitch. I might not do it now, or even a month from now, but it's gon' happen. I'm just giving you a heads up." She kissed my lips and moaned.

I gripped her ass and slid two fingers into her ass from the back, sliding them as deep into her as they could go. I kissed her lip before biting it. After I let it go, I continued to hold her with my face against hers. I spoke directly into her ear. "Princess, your emotions are running hot right now. All you can see is murder, and I understand that because I put that killer shit into you. But I'm letting you know right now that you ain't got shit to worry about. I would never choose anyone over you. As far as what she did to you, we'll address that at a later date, but I'm not gon' let you kill her, Princess. Ain't no reason to.

Trust me on that. We gon' get our shit together, get out of this country and move forward with our lives and live happily ever after."

She shook her head and backed off of my lap. "N'all, Taurus. I wish shit could be that simple, but it ain't. I got some things going on inside of me that can only be diffused with her death. This bitch could have killed me. She carrying your seed, and you got mad feelings for her. I can't take that shit. I'm too gone in the head over your ass. You got me this way. Now all I crave is murder. It's the only thing that makes sense to me right now. So, yeah, I'll be cool for a time. I'll play my role, and even flip this bitch with you. But when it's all said and done, I'm gon' get my revenge. You and this bitch got me scorned. And hell hath no fury like what's going on inside of me. I think it's best that I take this shit out on her when the time is right rather than take it out on you. Trust me on that." She ran her tongue across her teeth. "I ain't gon' fuck with her while she pregnant, but after she has that baby, all bets are off. Know that." She looked over my shoulder and bucked her eyes. "Here come these muthafuckas. Look, they can only hold me until tomorrow night, so make sure the following morning you're here to get me. I'm here 'cuz of that lie your mother made up to save that bitch Blaze. I can't wait 'til she have that baby."

I nodded. "I'll be here. Until then, you hold ya' head. Stay as low as possible. I love you, lil' mama."

The orderlies opened the big metal door and came in two deep. They stood behind Princess. Each grabbed an arm. "Sir, your visit is over. We're going to need for you to leave the premises after you check out with the front desk."

I nodded and looked over to Princess. She was mugging both men, one after the other. I didn't like the way they had her arms, but I knew we had to be cool. She only had one day to go.

She jerked her right arm away and frowned at the heavy-set orderly. "Say, bruh, you ain't gotta be grabbing on me so tight. I ain't going no fucking where."

"Oh, I'm sorry. Is this better?"

She sighed. "I love you too, Taurus. Remember, you better be here. No if, and's or buts."

Chapter 3

I'd decided to keep my mother, Jahliya and Blaze in the Hilton Hotel in Dallas. I got everybody their own Presidential Suite. My mother and Jahliya took one suite. Blaze took her own, and I had my own as well. I'd thought about having everybody stay in the same one, but then I thought about what would happen when Princess was finally released from the psych ward. I knew that she would throw a fit being in the same room with Blaze. I had to give her some time to calm down and get back used to things. Princess had a temper that was as horrible as mine. She was quick to kill, and she hated Blaze with a deadly passion. I knew she meant every word she'd spoken about bodying her after Blaze had my child. I didn't know what I was going to do yet.

Before I got to my suite, I knocked on the door to Blaze's room. She answered the door wearing a red and black, silk, Burberry robe. Her pregnant belly protruded. She was barefoot. Her pretty toes were French-tipped to match her fingernails. Her long hair was pulled back into a ponytail. She had a toothbrush in her mouth, brushing her teeth.

She looked into my eyes, rolled hers, and walked away from the door into the bathroom. I could hear her spitting in the sink. "You smell like pussy, Taurus. I get the visit with Princess went better than you thought it would." She scoffed and ran the sink water.

I closed the door behind me, sniffed under my arm, then my shirt. I couldn't smell anything, but I guessed females had the nose for that type of shit. I think I would have smelled another dude on either one of them right off the back as well. I cleared my throat. "Yeah, it did. She still pissed at yo' ass, too. I tried my best to talk some sense into her but she ain't going."

Blaze stepped into the bedroom portion of the suite and shrugged. "It is what it is. I'd be mad at me too. She gon' get enough of thinking it's so sweet with me. I know how to hold my own just like she do. Ain't no hoes over here, Taurus." She stepped back into the bathroom and threw me a drying towel. "Go jump yo' ass in the shower. Hurry up and come on out so we can talk and get an understanding. I got some things on my heart that I need to get off."

I took my shirt off, then unsnapped my bulletproof vest, dropping it to the floor. Before I could do the same with my pants, my phone buzzed. The face had dollar signs going across it. I knew that meant it was Hood Rich. I nodded at her, walked into the bathroom and closed the door. "What's good, Hood Rich?" I dropped my pants and ran the shower water; setting it to the right temperature. The bathroom smelled like Febreze. It was huge with a big vanity, a toilet, a bidet, a urinal, and even a Jacuzzi right outside of it. I sat on the closed lid of the toilet with my phone to my ear.

"Lil bruh, I need you to handle some business with me over here in Philly. I'm trying to get these streets right, and it's a few hotheads that are making it a lil' difficult, if you know what I mean." He paused so his words could sink in.

"How soon are you talking, 'cuz I still got a lot of shit to handle back here with my girls. I ain't had a chance to get us right just yet."

"Say no more. How about you let me get all of y'all situated out here in Miami? My mans got a few properties that he just laid down at my feet. Mansions. I'm sure the women will love that. I'll hand two over to you, no charge. You can do whatever you wanna do with them. You can let your girls fully furnish them, too. I'll take the hit. Long as after you get them right, you handle these Philly niggas with me and take that trip to Dubai. It's time I show you what this high life is all about. What do you say?" I could hear the sound of water crashing in his background. It sounded like he was on the beach or something.

"Yo, what about them Russian boys? You don't think we gotta shake the States altogether?"

After knocking off Nastia and her pops, I felt like we should have gotten as far away from the United States as possible. I knew firsthand that those Russians were nothing to play with. They show up at any time and do anything they wanted. If they could control the president of the United States, what power could a couple of dope boys like me and Hood Rich really have? We didn't stand a chance. I saw it. I wondered why he didn't.

"Lil bruh, right now, we're good. I got some shit in place that's gon' keep us from having to worry about them for a minute. You just let me handle my part and you get yourself in order so you can come and fuck with me. I owe you my life, dawg. You already know that. You gon' hurt a nigga heart if you decline these properties and help from me." He laughed, and there was a loud horn in his background followed the sound of screeching birds.

"Bruh, where you at right now?"

"I'm fucking around on this yacht I just copped. Cost me three-point-six million. I just found out that it takes a fucking million a year to keep it up and running. Everything cost, bruh. That's why we gotta turn this two tons of China into a billion dollars." He scoffed. "You got me talking all reckless and shit over this phone. Look, you gon' fuck with me or not?"

I closed my eyes and lowered my head. "Yeah, I need them mansions and you already know I ain't about to let you go at no nigga out east without having your back."

I could hear him clap his hand together one time real loud. "That's what the fuck I'm talking about. I'll give you a few weeks, and then I want you and your whole entourage to fly out in the jet to Miami. We'll get y'all squared away before you and I jump right on this business with these Philly niggas. We need that line. I'll be in touch, bruh. Love."

The line disconnected. I lowered my head and shook it. Then, I took the phone and set it on the vanity. Afterward, I stripped down and jumped into the shower, and stayed in it for a full half an hour.

When I got out of it, I draped a towel around my waist and made my way into the bedroom. Blaze was sitting in the middle of the bed, Indian style, reading her tablet. She had on a pair of Prada reading glasses. And as she read her tablet, her lips moved. I could hear the constant *pst pst pst* sound coming from them. When I stepped fully into the bedroom she looked up to me. I noticed that she'd hung my shirt on the back of a chair. My bulletproof vest was now in front of a fan.

She set the tablet down and smiled. "I cleaned that vest as best I could and sprayed some of that Febreze on it. You must get real sweaty under there, huh?"

I nodded and sat on the foot of the bed. "What's on your mind, Blaze?" I touched her left foot and ran my finger over the top of the pretty toes. I'd always been crazy about her pretty toes. There was nothing like a fine woman with pretty feet. It was my weakness. There had even been times when I'd thought that a female didn't look so good facially, but then I caught a glimpse of her toes and fingers and they were up to par. It changed how I saw her altogether.

She leaned to the side and set her tablet on the night table. She sat all the way back until her back was up against the headboard. "Taurus, what are you and I going to do?"

I climbed across the bed until I was sitting beside her. She smelled like Dior perfume. Her face looked a lil' shiny from my viewpoint. I figured she had one of her expensive creams on her face. Blaze had always been into beauty treatments and the latest fashions ever since I'd met her. She'd been a top-notch stripper ever since she'd stepped off the porch, being featured at major clubs all over the world. Before she stepped away from her career, she ventured out into the real estate world where she sold high-end property to celebrities all over the States. She was seasoned by all means.

"Going to do about what, Blaze?"

She flared her nostrils and rolled her head around on her shoulders. "Taurus, I'm not about to play these childish games with you. You know what I'm talking about." She adjusted herself on her left elbow, looking me over carefully.

I sighed. "Man, I just had this same conversation with Princess. I don't feel like having the same one all over again. But I guess we need to get an understanding."

She smiled. "Right. I think I deserve that. It's like I told you before, Taurus. I am more than willing to play my role. I love you with all my heart. But, I ain't trying to come between you and her. I know that you were technically with her before you were with me. It's just that this child changes everything. I can't be having this girl trying to come for me every second of every day when I have a kid to raise. If you are going to be with her, then be with her. But let me go. I don't want to be in the middle anymore, Taurus." She bit into her lower lip and exhaled, closing her eyes.

I peeled her robe open and laid my hand on her stomach, rubbing it in a circular motion. I kissed her right on the navel and laid my face on her warm skin. "You ain't going nowhere, Blaze. You knew what it was from day one, when you touched down in Memphis and found out she was my woman. You said you'd be cool with playing your role. I get we got a baby on the way and all of that, but why do things have to change so dramatically?"

She laughed to herself and shook her head. "I can't believe you said that. As smart as I've always painted you out to be, you are proving me so wrong right now." She looked at me and blew air through her teeth.

She got out of the bed with her robe wide open, exposing her naked body with her big belly protruding in front of her. Below, her kitty was shaved. Her thick thighs jiggled as she paced with her hands on her lower back. The curves of her inner breasts were on display by the gown's opening. She looked even sexier because she was pregnant. I couldn't believe it.

"Taurus, things have to change because we're going to be parents now. We have to be role models and show our child how two responsible human beings are supposed to act. What we're doing now is acting as if we're teenagers. Like we don't have a care in the world. That can't continue to go on. You got me and this girl trying to kill each other over you, and what if I had killed her, then what? What would you have done?"

I sat on the edge of the bed and exhaled. "Blaze, y'all ain't supposed to be fighting no way. Both of y'all knew what it was. Both of y'all. Now all of the sudden it's a problem. Everybody giving me ultimatums. I'm supposed to choose either you or her right here and right now. That's bullshit!" I snapped standing up. I grabbed my bulletproof vest and shirt off the back of the chair. I ain't feel like arguing with her or nobody else that night. I needed to chill; to rest my mind and come at things from a different angle the next day. My head was pounding.

Blaze walked over and took a hold of my wrist. "Taurus, you aren't going anywhere until we get this right. I get it, you're a street dude. You're probably not ready to settle down with one woman because you're still young. What you have to understand is that you are playing with real hearts now, though. Both of us are in serious love with you. The worst thing you can possibly do is play with a woman's heart. You will lose every single time. I promise you this." She looked at me for a long time, and then placed my hand on her stomach, looking into my eyes. "You feel that? That is why things have to get better."

I rubbed her stomach and swallowed. When I looked into her eyes I felt weak. Blaze had a way of getting through to me by the use of her wisdom. She knew how to make me get things on my own without her having to thoroughly spell them out. I always found myself falling more in love with her the longer we spent time alone.

I kneeled and kissed her stomach and rubbed my face all over it. "What am I supposed to do, Blaze? I feel lost right now. I love both of y'all. When I'm with her I feel like I can be with her for the rest of my life, and I can let you do your own thing. But then as soon as I get into your presence, I hunger for you, your style, the way you talk, your past, your wisdom. All of that makes me wanna snatch yo' ass up and never let you go. You are the woman that I've always seen myself marrying. Now we got this growing inside of you. I'm fucked up mentally. I can't lose you, and I don't want to lose her either. Why do things have to change?"

Blaze laid her hand on the top of my waves. "Baby, do you want me, or do want her? That's what it boils down to. You guys already have a daughter together. Your lives have been somewhat established. Y'all seemed to be doing just fine before I came back into the picture real heavy, right?" She held my face in both of her small hands, tilting it up so she could look into my eyes.

I shook my head and closed my eyes. "N'all, we got into a lot of bullshit, but it's good now." I kissed her stomach and stood up, looking down at her. "I ain't trying to lose you. I need you in my life more than ever. I can't imagine you not being here or raising our child with somebody else. It's my job to be there for you, and I'm doing it. So, you ain't going nowhere. I'd rather die than let you leave me. I gotta take care of you."

"But you don't though, Taurus. I got my own money. I got more than enough in the bank. Seven figures. I got properties all over Texas and California. Good credit, and I ain't never needed a man for nothing but sex. But I'm even over that. I'm to the point in my life where I want to feel happy and secure. I don't want to feel the way I do right now. I deserve so much more than the way I feel right now." She rubbed her hands down to my chest. "I think you should be with her, Taurus. She loves you, and she got that hood shit in her that I don't have. I'm going to go on about my business and figure life out. You don't have to worry about me anymore. I'll just—"

I don't know what came over me, but before she could finish what she was about to say, I snapped. I grabbed her by the neck and slammed her into the wall, holding on to it so tight that she could barely breathe. "Blaze, if you ever leave me, I'll track yo' ass down and kill you and our child." I tightened my grip again. "I love you too much to ever let you walk away from me. I ain't ready for that. You are my woman until I say you're not. You understand that?" I asked with my forehead against hers.

She slapped at my hand and nodded wildly. Her eyes were bugged out of her face. They were turning red. Her light caramel face was as well. I loosened my grip, and she let out a gasp of air. Falling to her knees, she was coughing with saliva dripping off of her lips. "Ahk! Ahk! What the fuck is your problem, Taurus? I couldn't breathe." She spat on the carpet and continued to hold her neck.

"I swear to God I ain't playing with you, Blaze. I love the fuck out of you, man. I need you more than you'll ever know, but you can't give up on me right now. Please."

She held her throat and slowly climbed to her feet. She stood in front of me and swallowed. "I can't believe that you actually did that. I never thought you would put your hands on me."

I felt guilty as hell that I had. I didn't know what had jumped into me at that moment. I guess I just saw what my life would be like without her in it, and I couldn't take it. As much as I loved Princess I still needed Blaze. She had a hold on me almost as powerful. "Damn, Blaze. Look, my bad. I ain't, mean to hurt you. I just ain't trying to have you going nowhere. You're my baby, and I need you. I—"

She stepped forward and kissed my lips, wrapping her arms around my neck. She kissed my lips hard, sucked on them, and ground her front into my towel. "I love you, Taurus. I love you so much. I ain't going nowhere. Whenever I say I am, just snatch me up like you did back there. She bit my lip and sucked on it again, moaning into my mouth, pulling my towel off. "You gotta give me some of this. I know you fucked Princess tonight and I don't even care. Just choke me a lil' bit and fuck me as hard as you can because I'm mad at you." She smacked my face and bit into my neck.

I trailed my hands below the small of her back and gripped her fat ass cheek. I slid my fingers in between them, all the way down to her soaking wet pregnant pussy. Juices ran down her thighs and over her ankles. I stood up and bent her over the bed, kneeling behind her. I licked all the way up her right thigh, and then the left. Her juices tasted salty and creamy. I stuck my nose into her pussy and inhaled deeply. Then I spread the sex lips with my thumbs and trapped her clitoris with my lips, sucking on it, scraping it with my teeth.

"Uhh-shit! Taurus! Hurry up and let me cum! Then fuck me, baby. I need it so bad." She whimpered, holding her ass cheeks apart for me.

I licked up and down her slit, swallowing her juices, sticking my tongue in and out of her tight pink hole while my nose rested on her asshole. I licked all around her anal ring and slid my tongue into it while pinching her clit.

"Aww-fuck, Taurus. I'm finna cum! I'm finna cum, baby. Keep eating me like that. Just like that!" She screamed with her face against the mattress.

While she came, I sucked on her clit, squeezing her sex lips together so all her juices could seep out of her and onto my tongue. She shivered, humping backward into my face. I stood up, climbed onto the bed, and laid her on her side. I picked her thick thigh up with my forearm while she rubbed my dick head up and down her oozing slit.

"Kill it, Taurus! Fuck me hard. Please." She scooted backward and impaled herself on my pipe, taking me whole.

I grabbed her throat and rocked forward with force, pulled all the way back and repeated the same motion, getting harder and harder with each thrust. She screeched under me. Her face was balled up. Her mouth was wide open. Her pussy felt like a hot, wet glove that tugged at me. Every time I pulled all the way back it was a little work sliding back into her hole. It oozed her essence in thick rivulets.

"Un! Un! Taurus! Taurus! Ahk! Ahk!" She moaned before I started to choke her harder, squeezing for a few seconds and releasing my grip. She forced her big booty back into my lap. It jiggled every time we made contact. My pipe slid deeper into her wetness. "Un! I'm yours, Taurus! I'm yours! Fuck me harder! Harder, baby!"

I bit into the back of her neck and sucked on it while my hips worked overtime, long-stroking that pussy. That pregnant pussy was awesome; soppy and wet. It was hotter than ever. I pulled on her hair and choked her once again, beating down her walls with my biceps bulging. "This my pussy, Blaze. This. Mine! You. Ain't. Going. No. Muthafucking. Where! You. Hear me!" I growled, speeding up the pace. I was fucking her so hard that all the pillows had fallen to the floor.

She curled her toes and threw her head back. "Aww-fuck! Yes! Okay! Okay, Taurus!" She bounced back into me, licking the arm that held her thigh up. "Yes!"

I curled my back and fucked her harder and harder, sucking all over her sweaty neck, putting a hickey on the thick vein that ran along the side of it.

"Aww! Taurus! Aww-fuck! Here I come again. Ooo-shit! Here I come, baby! Aww-a! Aww-a! Fuck!" She screamed, slamming back into me.

I grabbed a handful of her hair and bit into her neck while my hips continued to work. She squeezed the head of my pipe with her walls and it was too much. I grabbed her back to me roughly and came deep within her quivering pussy while she hollered that she loved me over and over.

Chapter 4

Instead of it only taking a week for me to get everybody ready to bounce to Miami, it took two because I kept having to stop Princess from going at Blaze. Every time she saw her somewhere in the house she'd drop whatever she was doing and would be frozen in place. Her hands would ball into fists, and the next thing I knew she was in her face ready to beat her into the ground.

Finally, two days before we were set to leave, my mother had all of us sit down in the living room. She turned the big smart screened television off and stood before us. Princess sat on the couch to my right and Blaze sat across from us on the love seat. Jahliya was out for the count, snoring lightly in the bed.

I was tired of them constantly arguing and beefing. They were always at each other's throats, acting as if they wanted to kill one another. Blaze was five months pregnant, and it was like the sight of her belly pissed Princess off more than anything else. So, I guess my mother felt like it was time to put an end to it.

She started off by taking a deep breath and sighing. "Look, y'all gon' have to stop all of this bickering back and forth. The fact is that y'all ain't the blame here, Taurus is. There is no way that two women in love with the same man can live under the same roof. It's just not possible. This ain't the olden days." She looked directly at me. "Taurus, you gon' have to choose one of them. You can't string both of them along. I raised you better than that."

Princess scoffed and snickered out loud. She shook her head and looked up to my mother. "Really? That's what you gon' start with?" She laughed and stood up. "Taurus, I love you. You are the father of my child, and I am thankful for that. I think you're an excellent father. I just wish you were a better man. Boy, you gon' have to choose which one of us you gon' be with. I know you don't think we about to live in the same mansion when we all get to Miami, 'cuz I ain't going. Ain't no way I'm finna live under the same roof with a bitch that tried to kill me. Excuse my language, mama, but I couldn't express that fact no other way. Now, if you plan on choosing her, it's good. I hear them niggas down in Miami fine as hell. I'm sure I can be snatched up by one of them." She laughed and looked down at me. "In conclusion, whatever choice you make, we gon' stick with it. That's all I got to say." She plopped down on the couch and crossed her thighs.

Blaze shook her head. "I'm too grown for all of this. Seriously, this is so high school."

"Well, bitch, why don't you bounce then? Make it easier on everybody else." Princess rolled her eyes and curled her lip.

Blaze laughed. "If it was up to me I would go on about my business, but Taurus ain't trying to let me go nowhere. Are you, Taurus?"

Princess snapped her neck and mugged me with hatred. "Oh, is that what it really is?"

My mother lowered her head and rubbed her temples. She waved us off and left the living room talking to herself.

I had a crazy headache at this point. "Look, I'm not droppin' neither one of y'all. Blaze, you knew what it was when you and I started fucking around again. Princess flat out told you that she was my woman and you were cool with that. You said you'd play your role, so that's what its gon' be. Far as you go, Princess."

"Yeah I wanna hear this shit." Princess said facing me. "Go 'head."

"You knew that Blaze and I had history. I was fucking with her before I was fucking with you. You and I just got real tight, real fast, but by that time, shawty was in my heart already, just like she is now. I ain't trying to lose neither one of you. I ain't making no decision either. Why should I?" I looked from one unto the other.

Blaze looked off into the distance. Princess sat there mugging me with seething anger.

"Bitch, you ain't gon' say shit to this nigga?" Princess asked Blaze. She looked like she wanted to jump off of the couch and attack her.

"I'd appreciate if you quit calling me out of my name, Princess. On the strength that you are a mother to his daughter, I try and refrain from disrespecting you. But you making it hard on me. I'm telling you that right now." Blaze said.

"Bitch, you making it hard on yourself. You letting this nigga do what the fuck he wanna do like it just don't matter. Where is your backbone?" Princess rolled her eyes.

Blaze snapped. "Where is yours? What is you about to do?"

Princess smiled. "I'ma show you right now. Taurus, you and her can have each other. I don't even wanna be with you no more. Fuck both of y'all. When we get to Miami, I'll take the mansion with your mother until I can get on my feet. Once I'm stable, I'm out. But you definitely gon' use some of them chips you got stacked up to get me right. I feel like half of all that shit is mine and Jahliya's anyway." She sat back on the couch, nodding with a big smile on her face.

I mean I could've stood up and fought with her, but I was tired. I couldn't see Princess going nowhere. I felt that Blaze would have left long before she did. So, I didn't really fight for her in this moment. I just let her have it. "Princess, like I said, I love you, and that shit ain't gon' change. If you feel like you don't wanna fuck with me no more after all we've been through, then so be it. We gon' get out here to Miami, and I'ma get you right. I'll invest in you in any way that you need me to. You ain't ever gotta worry about no paper no more, no matter what. As long as I'm breathing, you're straight, and so is Jahliya."

She stood up and waved me off. "Yeah, whatever, nigga. Like I said, I'm staying with our mother when I get down there. But as soon as my toes touch that dirt, I'ma be on my grind to make shit happen for me and my daughter. You do what you gotta do to get me right. You know how I am, so don't cross me more than you already have. That's not a threat, it's a warning like Cardi B advised." She looked over to Blaze. "You win." She walked out of the room and into the kitchen. I could hear her calling out to my mother.

Honestly, I felt sick on the stomach. I wanted to get up and snatch my lil' woman up and smack some sense into her. But at the same time, she had me heated. I never allowed for nobody to talk to me the way that she did. Princess was the only exception to that rule. Even when Blaze tried to get a lil' lippy, I'd put her in her place, ASAP. I think the reason I allowed for Princess to get down like she did was because she was so fucking small. I still couldn't believe how much heart she actually had.

Blaze came around the table and sat beside me. "Taurus, you sure you're going to just let her go like that? I mean, doesn't that hurt just a lil' bit?" She rubbed the side of my face and looked into my eyes, concerned.

I shrugged. "Maybe she just need a lil' space. It could be for the best. We need to focus on making sure that you deliver a healthy baby anyway." I kissed her on the forehead as I watched my mother and Princess talking in the kitchen.

She turned around and her and I made eye contact. She curled her lip and turned away from me. My heart was crushed.

***

We got to Miami early, Friday morning. When the Jet landed, Hood Rich had two stretch Cadillac Escalades pick us up from the airport. Hood Rich, Blaze and myself loaded into one. Jahliya, Princess and my mother loaded into the other one. I wanted everybody to get into the same one, but Princess' lil' evil ass wasn't having that. She started to make a commotion, and instead of getting into a big argument with her on the first day in a new place, I just let her have that victory.

We pulled into the Royal Land gated community just as Hood Rich handed me a bottle of Moet. He'd already popped the cork. "Taurus, this is the beginning of a new life for you and your people. I swear, they ain't gon' have no problems out here. I got this boy on lock. The security is crazy, and ain't nothing but professional basketball and football players that stay in this community." He sighed and puffed his jaws out. "Unfortunately, we got a lil' bit of a problem. I hope it ain't that bad though." He looked over at me and then out of the tinted window.

It was bright and sunny. I couldn't locate a cloud in the sky. We rolled past one big, beautiful mansion after the next. The lawns were well groomed. Almost each property that we passed had a gardener hard at work. Most had fountains in the middle of them. Long driveways led up to the palaces. They were two and three stories high. High-priced automobiles decorated the long driveways and garages that were opened for me to see. The entire area seemed intimidating yet intriguing. I'd feel good about moving my family here. It was a long way from the slums of Memphis.

I took a sip of the champagne. I really wasn't feeling it. It was too early in the morning to be getting tipsy. "So, what's the problem, Hood Rich?" I handed him back the bottle of Moet.

"I wasn't able to come through on one of the mansions. It's only one for now. I thought the homie was about to be traded to the Lakers, but he re-signed his contract for another two years. That fucked me. He good people though. There should be another crib opening up in like six months though. That'll be yours. I just need for you to make due until then. You think you can swing it?" He sipped out of the bottle.

I nodded, somewhat relieved. "Yeah, it's a blessing either way you look at it. So, I'm content. Might be a lil' drama for my baby mother, but she'll be alright."

Blaze scrunched her eyebrows. "Baby, you know it's about to be chaotic as hell up in there. How you know we ain't gon' wind up killing each other? You know how that girl is."

Hood Rich shook his head. "N'all, this one y'all going to has three levels, a pool house, twelve bedrooms, and four different sides of the place. Y'all don't even have to run into each other if you don't want to. All you gotta do is stay on the west side of the palace and she can stay on the east. It's two kitchens and five bathrooms. If you want, Taurus, I'll have my people come through and put up a wall or divider just so y'all can avoid that drama. It's up to you."

I wrapped my arm around Blaze. "Yeah, I just want my lady to have a healthy baby. That's all that matters to me right now. That and making sure my women are good at all times."

Hood Rich held up the bottle of Moet and smiled. "I got you, dawg. Trust me on that."

Ten minutes later we were walking into the foyer of the big palace. I had my arm around Blaze's lower back, sat our Gucci suitcases down on the floor, and looked around at all of the space before us.

The floors were marble, along with the countertops. There was a spiral staircase that led up to the other two flights of the mansion. Crystal chandeliers hung from the ceiling. I walked past the front portion of the mansion after seeing the big fireplace downstairs. Through the doors, I saw a big pool in the backyard. It looked to be about fifteen meters long. The sunlight reflected off its clear blue waters. I opened the door and saw the pool house in the back. A row of deck chairs led up to it. The pool had two diving boards right beside one another.

Blaze met me in the backyard and ran into my arms. "Baby, this place is huge. You sure we're going to be staying here?" She looked all around with a big smile on her face. She opened the door to the pool house and shrieked. The sun cast off her forehead. Her eyes were protected with Dolce and Gabbana sunglasses over her them. She ran back to me and hugged me tight.

I laughed and held her. "Yeah, we gon' be here for a minute until we can get our footing. After that we'll be able to get a few more of these. I'ma let y'all furnish it however you want to, too." I kissed her lips, sucking longer on the bottom one.

Princess stormed into the back where we were standing on the side of the big pool. She had a scowl on her face. She waited until she got about twenty feet away from us and snapped. "Taurus, you said it was supposed to be two of these. Why is your guy saying that this is the only one? That all of us will be staying here?" She stopped in front of us and looked up at me. Light traces of sweat peppered along her brow.

Blaze slid from under my arm and passed Princess. "I'll see you in the house, babe." She shook her head and walked into the patio doors.

"Princess, you need to calm yo' lil' ass down. This where we staying for right now. The other one fell through. So, unless you can do better, make the best of this shit. We ain't finna bring all that muhfucking drama to Miami. I'm letting you know that shit right now."

She sucked her teeth and stepped into my face. "Taurus, the only person bringing this drama is you. You said your mother and I was gonna have our own spot. That's what I expect. It was one of the only reasons I followed you and that bitch out here. You think I wanna be living under the same roof with you and that bitch? Watching y'all play house and shit?" She mugged me with mounting anger.

"I don't give a fuck what you want right now. This is what it is. So, either you gon' roll with it or do you. Ain't no locks on them doors to prevent you from going nowhere. Feel me?" I stepped past her on my way into the mansion.

She grabbed my arm and yanked so that I was facing her. "Nigga, what the fuck you think this is? You better check yo' self. You ain't talking to one of them bum ass bitches in the street. I ain't Blaze."

"That's it." I grabbed her by her neck and lifted her in the air. I carried her all the way into the pool house and flung her on the bed so hard that she bounced off of it and onto the floor.

She jumped up and ran at me with swinging fists, throwing haymakers trying to connect with any part of my face that she could. "Bitch ass nigga. I told you about putting yo' hands on me. I ain't one of these punk bitches on the street!" She screamed, going for what she knew.

I allowed for her to punch me three times in the face before I backhanded her ass over the bed. "Come on. Get yo' touchy ass up. Every time you hit me three times, I'm gon' give you one of these muhfuckas until you understand that you ain't running shit. Come on!"

She felt the corner of her mouth, looking at her fingers in search for blood and found none. "Aw, yeah. Aw, you hitting me now? A'ight, what's good, nigga?" She bounced on her toes, lowered her head and came swinging again.

She caught me in the jaw twice, and once in the lip. As soon as I felt that third hit, I blocked her next blow and slapped her back on the bed.

She kneeled over and slammed her fists into the comforter, hollering into the bed like a crazy person. "Aww! Fuck this shit!" She jumped up and looked around the room for a weapon. Her eyes fell on a broom that was lying beside the big aquarium. She rushed to it, grabbed it, and slowly walked back to me. "I got yo' big ass now, Taurus! You wanna buss my shit! Let's get it!" She swung the broom and crashed it into my forearm. Then, she cocked it back and hit me across the side of the head with it, then punched me square in the mouth. This knocked me back.

I stumbled into the wall, just as she raised the broom again, ready to bring the thick wood down on top of my head to finish me. I blocked it just in time with my forearm, breaking it in half. I grabbed her by the neck and slapped her across the face with so much velocity that it dazed her. She fell to one knee and swung the jagged wood at me. I blocked the assault and took both broken pieces out of her hand and brought her over my lap while I sat on the bed. I trapped her ankles with my own and pulled her Prada skirt above her waist, exposing her red thong.

Whap! Whap! I spanked her on the ass while she screamed and tried to punch at me unsuccessfully. Her ass cheeks turned a rosy shade of brown in a matter of seconds. "I. Told. You. That. You. Ain't. Running. Shit! You. Gon'. Fall. In. Line!" I tore that ass up.

After a few minutes, she gave in. "Okay, okay, Taurus! Fuck! Let me up! I get it! I get it, Daddy! Damn!" She wailed with her fists balled up.

Ignoring her, I gave her a few more hits, then released her to the floor. I was breathing hard and was still just as angry as before I'd started.

Princess sat on the floor looking up at me with tears in her eyes. Wiping them away, she stood up, pulled her skirt down and touched the corner of her mouth again and saw that there was blood. She swallowed and looked into my eyes. "A'ight, Taurus. We gon' do shit your way. You want us all to live under one roof. Cool, let's do it." A devilish grin appeared across her face as she touched the corner of her mouth once more. She looked down at her fingers and walked off. "Let's do it, Taurus."

I sat there on the bed for a little while with my head down, imagining the speck of blood that I'd seen on her fingers. I felt horrible. I never in my life thought that I would ever put my hands on a woman.

Especially not one that I loved. So many images of my father beating my mother when I was a kid flashed through my brain. With each memory, I became sicker and sicker until I was throwing up inside of the aquarium.

Chapter 5

Hood Rich tossed me a DSK with a thirty-round clip. "Look at that boy, Taurus. This one of them Dutch assault rifles. Real accurate and will knock a nigga head off with no hesitation. I just got a crate full of these muhfuckas from Cuba. We gon' need every last one of them to go at these Philly niggas 'cuz they play for keeps." He used his remote to turn on the projector that hung on the wall in the studio room of his mansion.

Hood Rich's mansion was three blocks over from the one he had given me. It was fully plush and so decked out that it made me want to step my game all the way up. He even had a baby white tiger that he had allowed to roam around the pad as if it were normal.

A picture of some project buildings came on to the screen. He pointed at them. "Those are the Diamond Projects of Philly right there. If we can break into these muhfuckas, we can make a million dollars a day off heroin alone. You already know what that Rebirth do. Now that that fool Meech is out of the equation we can turn up the way we're supposed to. Ain't neither one of us got no habits. I mean I fuck with Percocet and Oxys from time to time, but we ain't fucking with that Boy; that's the main thing. Anyway, the goal is to break into these projects and flood them with the Rebirth. That'll be seven million dollars a week from one sector of Philly. I'm thinking heading west as well and hitting up a few more hotspots. Do you know they got places in Philly that allow for the dope heads to do their dope in the open? They provide them with clean syringes, alcohol pads, and everything else they need to stay right. Everything except the dope. That's where we come in at. I wanna flood Philly. Then work my way over to Pittsburg. Get a bunch of that factory money."

He frowned and pressed on the clicker in his hand. It flipped to the next scene. A picture of a dark-skinned, heavy-set dude with long dreads. He had a red teardrop under his right eye and a mouth full of gold, with red diamonds on them. He looked menacing. His face was turned into a mug. He sat on the hood of a red Ferrari. Both doors were up.

"This nigga right here gon' be a problem. His name is Kilroy. He fuck with a group of killas that call themselves The Shooterz. These niggas are maniacs because of this fool right here. He recently lost his right-hand man. His name was Poppa. When he was alive, they were more about getting money. Now that he's gone, Kilroy became the leader of their deadly crew, and he broke the clique off into two sections. One side of The Shooterz are about getting the dope addicts to shoot their product into their veins. The other side is about slaying niggas like it ain't nothing. Kilroy got the Philly's law enforcement on his payroll. His arm stretches all the way out to New York and DC. Every major cat in the game that I ran across out east say he ain't the one to get involved with or cross. Fool's a savage. But you already know how we get down." He laughed.

I popped the clip out of the assault rifle and looked it over it before slamming it back into it. "I fucked around out east one time and never went back.

Them niggas out that way are grimy with no loyalty. Me and Princess had to slump one from her own bloodline, so I know what it is. Bruh, I'm down to do whatever you feeling, long as it help me to advance my people in every way." I cocked the DSK, looked through the scope, and pressed on the trigger, causing it to zoom into the spot on the wall that I had the scope focused on. I could actually see an ant crawling up it, and I was about a hundred feet away from it. I nodded. I liked that boy already.

Hood Rich picked up a bottle of Moet and sipped from it. "You know everybody got vices and someone who makes them weak. In Kilroy's case, he seem like he don't give a fuck about nothin' or nobody. So, if that's the case, his first love must be his money. Before we go at him directly, I wanna go at his paper supply. He got five, sixty thousand dollar a day Bandos on Troy Avenue in West Philly. We gon' tear them up and shake some shit up a lil' bit. This nigga thinking that he got Philly on lock. I wanna show him that he don't. After we fuck over Troy Avenue, I got some other shit up my sleeve. In the meantime, I'ma help you to get established out here on Baker Road, right behind South Beach. It's a heroin paradise right now. We gotta move some Haitians around, but it's good. Let's get this money, homie, before we hit up Dubai and let loose." Hood Rich leaned over and gave me a half-hug. "We roll out tomorrow. Let the women know we gon' be gone for about three days."

***

Blaze stepped out of the shower and started to dry her curly hair with the Prada towel. She stood on a drying mat, buck-naked, pregnant and fine as ever. I continued to line myself up in the mirror. My goatee was fuller now. I tried my best to keep it nice and neat at all times.

She dropped the towel, hugged my waist, kissed me on the back of the neck and smiled. "I love you so much, Taurus. I can't wait until our baby gets here. He gon' love you, too." She kissed my neck again, then walked out of the bathroom. She opened the dresser in the big bedroom, pulled out a pair of satin black panties, and stepped into them. Her titties had gotten fuller. They bounced on her chest. The nipples looked like pacifiers.

I stepped into the room and slid a black wife beater over my head. "Hood Rich say we gon' be out of town for like three days. We got some things we gotta take care out east. While I'm gone I just want you to lean back and relax. Maria is your maid. Anything you want or need she's been advised to take care of it for you. When I get back, I'ma take you out on the town so we can explore Miami a lil' bit."

She sucked her teeth. "Boy, I been to Miami before. If anything, I'ma give you a grand tour. I got plugs to the night life all over this place. You just try not to get too jealous when you see how they honor me out here." She smiled and walked over to me, wrapping her arms around my neck and looking into my eyes.

I rubbed all over that big booty. Her cheeks had swallowed the fabric. They were exposed on each side. I squeezed them and ran my finger all the way down to her crotch band. She spread her feet and moaned into my mouth with her eyes closed. Her crotch was already damp. Ever since she'd been pregnant it had been that way.

"I ain't gon' get jealous. I know who this body belong to. Just as long as you don't forget it. You hear me?" I bit into her bottom lip, sticking my teeth into it roughly before sucking it into my mouth.

She moaned and humped into me. "Mmm, will you miss me, baby?" She gripped my pipe and squeezed it in her little hand.

I moved her crotch band to the side from the back and rubbed over her wet lips, slipping two fingers deep into her bowl and worked them in and out in slow motion.

"I ain't gon' forget. This yours for the rest of my life. I love you so much, Taurus." She bounced back on my fingers, spreading her thighs further apart. Her back began to roll.

I sucked all over her lips. Her juices tasted so good to me. I pulled them out of her box, put both fingers on her lips and kissed her. Our tongues licked at the juices and my fingers. She licked up and down my fingers to taste more of herself. That drove me nuts and made me want to bend her over the big bed and fuck her until I couldn't get hard no more. Before I could, there was a pounding on the door. I fed my fingers to Blaze and allowed for her to suck them clean before I squirted Purell into the palm of my hand and rubbed it around.

When I opened the door, Princess stood before me with Jahliya on her hip. "It's like five trucks downstairs with all of the stuff we'd ordered to fill this empty ass place up. Can I give them permission to come in and set it up?" She asked, looking over my shoulder into the bedroom. I detected a hint of jealousy in her eyes, but of course she played it off like an actress.

I nodded. "Yeah, go ahead. But while they're doing their thing, you and I need to talk real quick so I can let you know what's good. That cool?"

Jahliya reached for me and I took her off of Princess' hip. I popped a piece of gum into my mouth then kissed my daughter on the cheek while she laughed at the top of her lungs.

"Taurus, long as it ain't got nothing to do with that girl in that room, we're good. I swear to God I don't feel like going down that road right now." She walked off and headed down the stairs.

I stepped into the room and closed the door behind me. "Baby, the furniture people are here. Princess say its plenty trucks downstairs. You need to get dressed so you can tell them where you want everything."

Blaze gave me a frustrated look as she clicked her bra in place. "Baby, I was hoping that I could get some real quick before you be gone for three whole days. You don't think I can get like five quick minutes. Please? I need it so bad." She bit into her bottom lip.

My mother knocked on the door and stuck her head in. "Y'all know all the stuff we ordered has arrived. Y'all better come tell these men where y'all want everything set up." She warned.

"Mama, can you take Jahliya for one second. Me and Taurus need to talk real fast before we come downstairs. It won't take longer than five minutes, I promise." Blaze clasped her fingers together in prayer fashion.

My mother nodded. "Yeah, sure. Give her to me, baby. But y'all better hurry up."

Jahliya damn near threw a temper tantrum as my mother pulled her from my arms. She held on to my shirt and ripped the collar. "Daddy. Daddy. I don't wanna go!" She screamed until my mother closed the door behind them.

Before I had the chance to feel guilty about handing my child over to my mother, Blaze locked the door, jogged over to the bed and laid on her side. She lifted her right thigh and pulled her panties to the side, exposing her juicy pussy that leaked clear gel. "Come on, Taurus. Hurry up. Please, baby." She slid two fingers into herself.

I rushed over and placed her ankle on my shoulder after lowering my pants and boxers. Already throbbing in anticipation, I slammed into her box and started to kill that shit while she pulled on her engorged nipples. She licked at them.

"Yes! Yes! Yes! Fuck me, Taurus! Yes! Ooh, shit!" She mumbled as I killed her super wet pussy with long strokes, pinching her clit the whole time.

I clenched my teeth, loving the way her titties looked as they shook on her chest. Blaze was bad. I was thankful I'd popped a baby into her. I needed to have tabs on that pussy for the rest of my life. It was that good. I was trying to kill it right then— gripping her thigh and pulling her to me so I could hit her bottom.

Her eyes rolled into the back of her head. A trace of drool slid down her cheek as her head bounced back and forth on her neck. "Here it come. Here it come. Aww fuck, here it come, baby!"

I rubbed her clit in wild circles as I plunged into her harder and harder. She came all over my thrusting pipe, seconds before I splashed into her gut. After we finished, we both jumped up and got our hygiene together.

***

Princess pointed to the empty wall. "Yeah, I want that big boy right up there," she told the delivery man. She'd been walking around giving out orders the whole time I'd been trying to talk to her, and it was pissing me off.

The delivery man smiled. "You're going to love this television, ma'am. It'll make it feel like you're acting inside of it. You'll see." He walked away with a smile on his chubby face.

I grabbed her wrist. "Shawty, did you hear what the fuck I said?"

"Ooh, daddy. You said a swear word." Jahliya chastised. I was holding her in my arms. She laid her head on my shoulder after telling me what I'd done wrong.

"Baby, I'm sorry. I didn't mean to. I'll try and be better, okay?" I kissed her cheek and then all over her Princess-looking face. The only things I'd passed on to her were my deep dimples and eyes. Other than that, she was Princess' twin.

"I heard you, Taurus. You gon' be gone for three days with Hood Rich. Y'all finna go and handle some business out east. What do you want me to say? I ain't keeping tabs on you no more. That's Blaze's job." She rolled her eyes and yanked her wrist away from me.

I don't know why that cut me so deep, but it felt like she'd stabbed me in the heart with a knife. I stood there for a second holding my daughter, then walked up behind her and grabbed her wrist again. She'd been directing the delivery men on where she wanted her washer and dryer set up.

She sighed and looked up at me as if she were drained. "Now what, Taurus? Jesus Christ, you are getting on my nerves."

Had I not been holding, Jahliya I would have snatched her lil' ass up and got at her a lil' bit. But I vowed to never go there with Princess in front of our daughter. Jahliya had been through enough already. We owed her more than that.

"Look, I'm just making sure you know what's good. Will you need anything while I'm gone?"

Jahliya kissed my cheek and wrapped her little arms around my neck, hugging me tight.

"I definitely ain't about to be cooped up in this house. I'm trying to see what's good with Miami because I ain't ever been down here before. So, you can leave me with like twenty thousand, so I can splurge a lil' bit." She held out her hand.

"I got you. Just make sure that you spend some of that on Jahliya. She need some new clothes. It's a whole different culture down here so we gotta make sure that she'll be up to par." I kissed my daughter's cheek again and caressed her silky hair that were in barrettes.

"That the case, I'ma need thirty 'cuz that twenty is for me. My name ain't Princess for nothing."

In the end I wound up giving her just what she asked for.

I caught my mother coming down the long hallway carrying a dehumidifier in her hands. When she saw me, she walked up to me and pecked me on the lips. "Hey, baby. You and Princess finally done arguing in front of my grandbaby?" She frowned.

I nodded and hugged her. "Yeah, it's good now. But you know how she is." I exhaled and shook my head. "Anyway, I'ma give you this lil' ten thousand just in case you need anything while I'm gone. I'ma be out for three days. Make sure Princess don't do nothing crazy to Blaze."

The movers were all over the mansion like bugs, carrying different appliances and furniture pieces. More than once we had to move out of the way, so they could get past.

She nodded. "I'll do my best, baby. I don't like seeing them argue the way they do either. It ain't right for Jahliya to witness that. Plus, we can't bring this other baby into the world with all of that chaos. You're killing them girls though, Taurus. Princess told me that you put your hands on her and I couldn't believe it. Out of all of my children, I would have never thought you'd be that one." She rubbed the side of my face.

I took her hand and lowered it. "She ain't the average female, mama. You know she ain't. That girl is looney. The only way I can get through to her is if I communicate in the only way she understands me. And that's messed up."

"Baby, there is nothing a woman can do that will justify you putting your hands on her. She's hurt.

Her heart is broken down the middle, and the only way she knows how to get you to feel what she is feeling internally is to cause you physical pain. But no matter how much of it she causes it will never amount to a tenth of what her heart is feeling right now. Believe me."

I ran my hand over my face in defeat and felt horrible. I knew that she was right. I looked over her shoulder, and me and Princess caught each other's eye again. She held mine for a long time before directing another delivery man on where to set up the entertainment system.

"Mama, what should I do? How do I get things in order with these two? I love the both of them a lot."

My mother held my face with both of her small hands. "Listen to me, son. A man cannot have his cake and eat it, too. If you continue doing what you doing, those girls are going to decide for and I can guarantee, it will hurt you for the rest of your life. Hell hath no fury like a woman scorned. You have to understand that." She kissed my cheek. "Thank you for the money. Be safe and get home soon. Your presence is needed."

Chapter 6

We arrived in Philly the next night at about nine o'clock, there was a light drizzle of rain coming from the sky, as me and Hood Rich chilled in the back of the Lincoln Navigator being driven by one of his Point Men. "Yo, Hood Rich, I'ma swing y'all by the Diamond Projects real quick so y'all can see how son 'n 'em get down. Word is bond, rain, snow, sleet or hail, kid 'n 'em be out getting them ends." Quik said, looking over his shoulder at us. He was dark-skinned with gray eyes. He had a bald head with bumps all over his face. He drove with a Tech 9 on his lap.

In the passenger's seat was another one of Hood Rich's Point Men, Blast. He was skinny, also bald headed, with an eyepatch. Both had Techs on their laps and scanned the streets as we rolled down them on high alert. Behind us were two black vans full of Gunners. These were savages that were ready to buss if they saw anything out of the ordinary. Then, there was one in front leading traffic. Each van had eight men, heavily armed and about that life.

I had a DSK on my lap with a thirty-round magazine, and so did Hood Rich. I was on point, and Princess had me so heated that I was ready to smoke something. I needed to spill some blood, and real soon too. It had been a minute. At least that's how I felt.

"Look, Taurus, I want you to pay close attention to how these niggas run they operation, too. That way, once we take over this bitch, we won't change nothing. The goal is to not take this shit out on the hypes 'cuz it ain't their fault. We gotta remove the pushers and keep the same system in place. Normalcy is equivalent to consistency for anybody that got a habit. Most feens would be happy if every day was Ground Hog Day, as long as they was able to get high as a kite." He frowned.

I nodded. "I already know that, bruh. This life flow through my veins and beat in my heart. This ain't the first hood I done took over." Sometimes I felt that Hood Rich had a habit of trying to lace me like I was one of those niggas that didn't understand the game on every single level that he did. In my opinion, the only thing he had over me was that foreign shit. He was handling business all over the world and I'd only been confined to the United States.

He put his hand on my shoulder. "I know you're real sharp, Taurus, but it's just my way. You're my right hand now. It's my job to make sure that we're on the same page at all times. You feel me, bruh?"

I nodded. "No doubt. I got you."

We pulled a block away from where the Diamond Project buildings started. Even from that distance I could make out long lines of dope addicts, waiting to be served. Way up toward the Projects there were about seven dudes walking up and down the line with their hands under their shirts, making sure that the line stayed straight and orderly. They barked their orders with half masks covering their faces. They had a cocky swagger to them.

In the parking lot of the Diamond Projects were three different groups of ten men. They had on puffy coats with half masks over their faces. Every time a feen went into the buildings, one of them followed them inside, and another brought out the hype that was taken inside before that one. I saw that there were two specific Benz trucks rolling back and forth on the street in front of the Projects as if on security. There were big cinder blocks blocking cars from driving into the parking lot of the buildings. To get into the parking lot, you had to pull up and wait for one of the security men to come to your whip and look inside of it. They did this with their guns pointed at the driver and another of the security team had his pointed at the passenger. One you were cleared to roll through, two of them ran out and moved a series of cinder blocks so you could pass. It was as hard to get out as it was to get in.

"Now you see what I'm saying, Hood Rich. It's gon' be like trying to get in between a nun's legs, Kid. Word is bond. That nigga Kilroy got drones flying all around the Projects filming his shits. The footage goes right back to the headquarters of the Shooterz. These niggas making a million dollars a day, Son. They got technology that we can't begin to understand." Quik said shaking his head and mugging the Project buildings.

I laughed. "We got this nigga, bruh. I don't give a fuck how they getting down or how secure they think that muhfucka is, where I come from we make nuns open them thighs and buss that shit wide open. For a million a day, we'll take over the White House." I curled my upper lip as I watched the niggas in action.

Hood Rich eyed them just as close. "Just let me and my lil' nigga worry about how we gon' break into that bitch. Y'all keep your ear to the streets. Stay loyal, and when we do what we need to do, I'll make sure that you and your niggas are eating on a bigger plate than Kilroy ever had. That's my word."

"We already know your word is bond, Hood Rich. You can expect nothing less than our loyalty. Word to my mother." Blast nodded.

"That's all I ask. Give me that and everything else will fall right into place," he assured, mugging the Project building.

***

Later that night, we hit up a club by the name of Rubies. It was located in West Philly right on the boulevard. I followed Hood Rich's directions and parked the money green Porsche in the back of the club where there was a small parking lot that could only fit about four cars. I wanted to ask Hood Rich why he wanted to have me park there, but I decided to roll with it. Especially since before we left the hotel he asked me three different times if I was wearing a bulletproof vest. Each time I told him that I was.

I turned off the ignition to the Porsche and removed the seatbelt. It was eleven o'clock at night, and the club's parking lot was packed. Where we'd parked there had only been one space left. It was hot and humid. There were like a million mosquitoes flying all around the car. About ten feet away from my driver's door were two dead cats. Both had maggots crawling all over them. One of the cats were missing fur on its head. It was completely gone. The maggots crawled all over the skull. It looked crazy.

I took my .40 Glock from under the seat and slid it into the small of my back, then slid the .380

into my ankle. Hood Rich kept on saying that the niggas in Philly were grimy. I wasn't trying to let none of them niggas get the ups on me. As far as I was concerned, everyone that I saw was an enemy.

Hood Rich loaded up and made sure that his vest was secure on his torso. "Taurus, we going in here so I can sit down and holla at this nigga Pancho. He one of the old heads that got a lil' pull in West Philly somebody breathed on the nigga, and now he sent word to me about the whole Diamond Project ordeal. I'm letting you know now that even though I'm about to sit down and holler at him, by the end of the night, we gon' body this punk. I dropped a few chips to the owner and he know what's good. All these Philly niggas understand is money. Stay on point and don't hesitate to buss your gun. Oh, they gon' pat us down at the door, but that's taken care of too. Just roll with it." He opened his door and stepped out into the night.

I did the same. It smelled like spoiled garbage and fish in the air. Dogs barked off in the distance. Somebody was blaring their music coming down the busy street. It made the ground rumble. There was a line standing in front of the club, but we by passed it and made our way to the front of it, much to the dismay of the patrons waiting to get inside. I could hear them murmuring and sucking their teeth loudly. I looked over my shoulder a few times and saw how we were mugged with hatred from both men and women. The smell of cheap perfume carried into the air, along with cigarette smoke and alcohol.

When we got to the front of the line, a big, bald headed, dark-skinned dude who looked like he ate whole animals for sport stepped up to Hood Rich and held his hand out. Hood Rich slapped it away and looked him up and down. I slid my hand toward my lower back, ready to grab that .40 and blow his shit back if need be.

"Say, get yo' fucking hands off me, homey. You don't know me like that." Hood Rich flared his nostrils.

The big bodyguard frowned. "You gotta be on the list. Nobody passes me without being on the list. What's the name?"

"Hood Rich, nigga. I'm Willie's guest. The owner."

The giant looked down his tablet until he found Hood Rich's name. "Here you go right here. Party of two. A'ight, you good to go." He held his mouth piece to his lips and said something into it.

I couldn't hear him because I was too busy scanning the crowd for potential enemies. All of them looked as if they hated us for holding the line up. I could tell that I wasn't gon' like Philly. I wanted us to handle our business and get the fuck up out of there.

The second bodyguard came out and ushered us to the doorway of the big club where he patted us down. Hood Rich went first. I knew for a fact that Hood Rich had three pistols on him, so after I saw that the big guard didn't recover either one of them from him, I knew I was good. He came over and patted me down next. He did the same thing that he did to Hood Rich before he told me that we were both good to go.

Three minutes later we were squeezing our way through the packed dance club. J. Cole's "King of Diamonds" played out of the speakers loudly. Everywhere I looked there was a thick ass female twerking like her life depended on it. Some had their hands on the floor, really getting it in. The club smelled kind of musky. There was plenty weed smoke in the air, so much so that I got a contact before we even made it upstairs to the second level of the club. After we passed the velvet ropes that were at the bottom of the staircase along with another big body guard, we were led to a room way off at the end of the level.

Standing in front of the room door was a tall, light skinned man with graying cornrows. He shook hands with Hood Rich and patted him on the back. "Long time no see, brother."

Hood Rich shook up with him and nodded. "Yep. This my family right here. He about to be the King of Miami; trust an believe that. His name Taurus."

I wasn't with all that handshaking shit. I was a real germaphobe, so I just nodded at him. "What's good, bruh?"

He extended his hand, then turned it into a fist so he could dab mine after he saw me do the same thing. "A'ight, lil' bruh." He turned to Hood Rich. "Pancho in there along with his son. I already know what it is. When you're done, come out of this room and go into that one right there. Inside of that room is a backdoor that leads to a flight of stairs that goes straight out the back door. After you do your thing, use that route. I'd appreciate it if you took them niggas with you, but it is what it is. I got a clean-up crew." He laughed.

Hood Rich curled his lip. "For fifty gees, you better. Not to mention the four bricks of that good-good. You should be handling this business for me." He turned his back on him and looked over to me. "Let's go and take a good look at these niggas, Taurus." He waved Willie off.

We stepped into the room. It was decorated with red leather sofas and had a big screen television hung up on the wall. It was turned to the Philly versus Celtics NBA game. There was a table with all types of soul food on it stationed right behind the leather sofa. In front of the couch was a wooden table that had a bucket of ice with two bottles of Moet in them. The table separated the two leather sofas. On the sofas sat Pancho. He was a dark-skinned man with red eyes and long graying dreadlocks. He was sipping from a twenty-four ounce can of Old English. He was dressed in all black with a black bandana around his neck. To the right of him, and with a mug on his face, was his son Lil' P. He was just as ugly as his father and slightly more muscular. Both had gold teeth and blood shot eyes.

I closed the door and then sat down a few inches away from Hood Rich. I looked the men over closely to try and see what vibe I got from them.

Pancho took a bottle of Moet out of the bucket of ice and handed it to Hood Rich. "You gon' introduce me to your sidekick?"

Hood Rich shook his head. "N'all, you don't need to know my nigga name. What you wanna talk about? Time is money."

"Watch how you talking to my pops, nigga." Lil' P said, acting like he was getting ready to jump up.

As soon as he would have I was getting ready to fill his ass up with a bunch of holes. I could already taste the kill. "Bruh, you can take that hostility out of your voice. You ain't on shit with my big homie right now." I said, mugging this fuck nigga.

He frowned and looked me up and down but didn't utter another word. It was in his best interest, too.

Pancho held his hand up and never took his eyes off of Hood Rich. "Chill out, son. It's good. This just how them niggas from Chicago communicate." He sucked his gold teeth and continued to mug Hood Rich. "I received word that you're thinking about moving in on the Diamond Projects. If that's so, we need to nip that shit in the bud right now. Me and my crew got dibs on that before any outsiders do." He sucked his teeth again.

Hood Rich popped the cork on the Moet and licked the fizz that spilled out of it. "Nigga, you been in Philly for damn near forty years still peddling the small quantities. If you ain't had the heart, or the will power to take over the Diamond Projects yet, then you never will." He laughed. "You know what happens to niggas that fuck in my business when they ain't supposed to, right?" Hood Rich grabbed the other bottle and handed it to me.

I took it and set it on the side of me. I was still mugging Lil' P. I felt some type of way around this nigga. I don't know what it was.

Pancho nodded. "I saved your life, Hood Rich. Them niggas was getting ready to shank yo' ass up, and had it not been for me you'd be a dead man right now. You told me that you'd stay out of Philly. That was the deal. What has changed?"

Hood Rich took a long swallow from the bottle of Moet and scoffed. "Them DC niggas was about to hit me up because I rotated around the compound with you. That beef ain't have shit to do with me until it did. Once they tried me, that was the last time anybody did. Taurus, my niggas from Chicago, left so many of their heads cracked open that they put the joint on lockdown for three months. Upon further investigation, it turns out that ol' Pancho over here had ripped a few of the niggas off before he'd gotten indicted. They knew he wasn't on shit but saw him kicking it with me. The law of the joint says you gotta cut the head off the snake, so the body will die. I was the head. This stud was supposed to be a part of our body. But you wasn't doing shit but looking for protection after these Philly niggas abandoned you." Hood Rich said, sucking his teeth now.

Pancho looked over to Lil' P to see his reaction. Then, to me, and finally back to Hood Rich. "Hood Rich, you one of the cockiest niggas I've ever met. You think Kilroy about to roll over for you so you can take his buildings? You outta yo' fucking mind. That fool crazier than anybody you've ever dealt with. I'm willing to put money on that. You and yo' nigga ain't gon' do shit but leave in a body bag." He laughed and looked Hood Rich in the eye.

"Yo, Pops, these niggas ain't on nothin'. Let's get up out of here before I wind up smoking one of these fools." Lil' P curled his upper lip and continued to mug me with hatred. His right hand had slid under his shirt.

Pancho shook his head. "N'all, not before I get an understanding with Hood Rich, son. I know how this fool's mind works. He been state to state taking over hoods and shit. But he ain't ever met the likes of us Philly niggas. Hood Rich, the next muthafucka that's gon' have the Diamond is me and my crew. We bleed Philly, nigga. Kilroy got me seeing two hundred gees a week. It's the only reason I ain't moved on him. All I gotta do is—"

"Only reason you ain't moved on him is because you a bitch. And that gangsta shit ain't in you." Hood Rich took another sip from the bottle of Moet and smiled.

"It's in me though, nigga!" Lil' P came from under his shirt and bussed Hood Rich twice in the chest. *Boom. Boom.* Fire spat from the barrel of his .38 Special and lit up the room in two quick flashes. "Fuck nigga!"

I swung the bottle of Moet that Hood Rich had given me and crashed it right on the side of his forehead, cracking it wide open. I then jumped up and kicked him in the chest. He flew over the back of the couch. His gun slid across the floor toward the closed door.

Pancho reached under his shirt and came up with a long .357 revolver. It was so long that by the time he got it out of his pants, my .40 Glock was out and cocked.

I aimed it straight at his face and fucked the trigger four quick times. *Boom. Boom. Boom. Boom.* "Bitch ass nigga!"

The bullets slammed into his face and knocked chunks of it away before he twisted and fell backward on the table. I reached over the couch and gave Lil' P three to the side of the head. Before he could rise from his push up position his brains were leaking out of his head.

"Memphis, nigga!"

Hood Rich patted at his vest. He dug his fingers inside of the holes and picked the slugs out of them before sucking his fingers into his mouth. He struggled to get off of the couch. I had to help him up. "Let's get the fuck out of here, Taurus. We got a lil' more work to do. These Philly niggas don't know who they fucking with." He put his arm around my neck, and I guided him to the door.

As soon as we opened it, four of Willie's men rushed in past us with black garbage bags and chainsaws. We followed the same flight plan that Willie had given us. Two minutes later we, were back in the Porsche, headed to another part of west Philly.

Chapter 7

Hood Rich stood in the alley in front of the Porsche's headlights with his shirt off. He'd thrown his used vest to the concrete, rubbing his fingers over the places where the slugs had burned him. "Fuck, Taurus. I'm sick of niggas hitting me with these hot ones. Thank God for that vest though." He shook his head. He rubbed an alcohol pad all over the spots, then slid a black wife beater over his head, and a new vest. After those were in place, he buttoned up his Tom Ford and got behind the wheel of the Porsche, slamming the door.

I looked all around the alley for predators. I was on high alert. I didn't like Philly for one second. I know I keep saying that, but it's the truth. I had an eerie feeling the whole time I was in the city. I knew my body count was going to be through the roof by the time I left.

Hood Rich reached under his seat and sat one of the DSKs on his lap. I wish I could think that we were done with this beef shit for the night, but we were far from it. I ain't taking no more slugs, that's for damn sure. He started the ignition and peeled out of the alley.

"What's good? Where are we headed?" I looked over to him with my .40 on my lap. After clapping Pancho and his son I felt a lil' better. It had been a while for me. I'd been going through so many mental battles with Princess to kill up some shit just to ease my nerves. I was ready for whatever Hood Rich had in mind.

"We finna catch this nigga Boscoe slipping over here on King Drive. I just got a text from one of my Point Men that him and a bunch of his niggas is having a lil' get together for his baby mother. It's her thirtieth birthday. My mans gon' let us in through the backdoor. We gon' hit up every nigga in there and let 'em know that we're here. Boscoe is Kilroy's right-hand man. You see, I wanna rattle Kilroy before we knock his head off and break up his operations. You gotta fuck with a nigga's head if you really wanna conquer them. I want this nigga to be so discombobulated that he can't even think straight. Once that happens, we gon' move forward to the next plan. I'ma show you some shit that's gon' blow your mind. Everything that I'm doing has a purpose. Trust me, lil' bruh."

I nodded as he pulled onto the highway. "I don't understand why we don't go straight at dude. We got stupid money. We can send some send offs directly at him about fifty deep, heavily armed. Then we can clean up any mess that they leave behind. We having too much money to be getting our hands dirty, don't you think?" I pulled a blunt out of my inside pocket and sparked the Tropical Loud that I'd copped from my plug in Memphis. Two pulls from it and I was lit already.

"This shit personal, Taurus. That nigga Kilroy murdered my lil' cousin, Jayden, while he was in Atlanta. After he killed him, he stripped him of more than four million dollars in cash and smoked my two female cousins. It'll be easy to let some other niggas handle this business, but I want this shit for myself, and I wanna share it with you. I guess I'm crazy like that. I should have my ass in London right now, but I had to put that shit on hold until I finish this shit back here. It's my vice. I love getting my hands dirty when it's personal."

I inhaled four string pulls and handed him the stuffed blunt. "Dawg, for what it's worth, if a muhfucka smoked somebody in my family I'd have to handle my own business too. You can't enjoy it unless you're the one that's sending them to the Reaper, so I feel you on that." I scanned the highway and laid my head against the headrest. I was high as hell. My eyes were low, yet fully focused.

"That's why I fuck with you the long way, Taurus. It's 'cuz you're just like me in a lot of ways. You got heart, and you're a thinker. I'ma make sure that after all of this business is done that you're in the best possible position to support your family for a long, long time. Big bruh making moves with people that you wouldn't even believe I am. If I continue to play my cards right, we gon' have a plug in the White House in a matter of months." He inhaled deeply and passed the blunt back to me. "That shit sound farfetched don't it?" His voice was strained because he was holding the weed smoke in.

I activated the massage controls on the passenger seat and relaxed. I shrugged. "Bruh, I can't even begin to understand what level of the game you're at right now. You been going hard since back when my old man was a king pin, so I can't doubt you. I can only wish you the best because whatever you're doing will ultimately benefit me and mine."

Hood Rich nodded. "Long as you know that to be what it is, we'll always be on the same page. I got a lot of love for you, bruh. We gon' do it big in Dubai. We got to. I'm plugged in all of the hot spots." He pulled onto an exit ramp after hitting his blinkers.

"I can't wait either, bruh. But for now, let's fuck over this city and get up out of here." I grabbed my DSK from under my seat and put my .40 in the small of my back.

***

Rain began to drizzle from the sky. Lightning flashed overhead. The wind picked up its speeds, and the thunder roared. In a matter of seconds, the rain was coming down full-on. It was pitch black in the backyard. About forty lighting bugs flew across it, flashing their lime green bottoms. I placed my shoulder against the back of the house, just as the backdoor opened and out stepped a high yellow dude with a long perm. He popped his hood over his head and looked back into the house before closing the door behind him. I could hear loud music blaring from inside. It also smelled like they were cooking.

Hood Rich snatched him by the jacket and held him up against the side of the house. "What the fuck took you so long, nigga?"

The yellow man shook his head. "I had to make sure everythang was everythang, Hood Rich, damn. I couldn't have you walking into no trap." He swallowed as the rain began to storm. It was coming down so hard that it felt like hail.

"How many people in there right now? You better be precise, too?"

"I am. It's ten people. Boscoe and four of his dudes. Three females and two kids. They upstairs sleep. Boscoe's daughter is babysitting them. She's twelve. They got the stereo system in front of the front door because it's the only three-prong outlet in the house. Everybody been using the backdoor to come and go as they please. We can't be back here all day. We good?"

Hood Rich nodded. "Yeah, we good. Tell that fuck nigga Kilroy what it is. Let 'em know he living on borrowed time. Now get the fuck out of here," he ordered.

The yellow dude got ready to run past me and I grabbed him by the throat and put my DSK to his forehead. "What? We finna let this nigga live? Since when?" I asked with my finger on the trigger. Hood Rich had said that we were going to kill the whole house. I couldn't understand why we'd allow for this yellow dude to walk away scot free. That seemed stupid to me.

"Man, Hood Rich, call off your dog, man." He whimpered.

That made me want to slay him even more. There was nothing that I hated more than a soft ass nigga. I felt that all of them deserved to be bodied. I tightened my grip on his neck.

Hood Rich waved me off. "Let him go, Taurus. He ain't no threat. I need him to get word back to Kilroy. That's important."

I shook my head. "Bruh, that's stupid. I don't know what you thinking, but I can't let that happen. The code of the streets prevent me from doing that." I slammed the butt of my DSK into the yellow dude's forehead.

He fell backward, but before he could fall on his ass, Hood Rich snatched him into a choke hold.

"You gotta trust me, Taurus." He said through clenched teeth, squeezing the yellow dude's throat tighter and tighter.

His eyes bugged out of his head as the rain splattered into his face. He smacked at Hood Rich's arms, gagging. I didn't want this murder to take all day. I cocked back and punched him as hard as I could in the gut, knocking the wind out of him. Lightning flashed across the sky before thunder roared loudly. Hood Rich choked him out for a full five minutes before dropping him to the ground. I kicked his body up against the bottom of the fence that separated the house we were about to go into from its neighbors.

There was a heavy scent of fried Perch Fish in the air. I detected Spaghetti as well. My stomach growled. I hadn't eaten anything since that morning. Me and Hood Rich had been ripping and running all over Philly.

A van pulled up in the back alley. Four dudes got out and jogged in our direction with masks on their faces. My first instincts were to air they ass out. Had the one in front not yelled Hood Rich's name I would have.

Hood Rich laid his hand on my shoulder. "It's good, bruh. That's Quik and his crew. I called them to make sure that nobody gets out of this house." He shook up with Quick.

Quik gave him a half of hug and then handed him a small Ziploc bag that had two silencers in them. "I got here as fast as I could. Got a bunch of crashes out there. But that's what you asked for. They'll fit right into them DSKs." He looked up at the house and snickered. "They in there having a gay ol' time. Don't even know what's about to happen to them."

I slid my Scream mask over my face. Hood Rich had a Donald Trump mask.

He wiped the rain off of his face and slid it on. "Bruh, all I need y'all to do is guard them exits. Don't put a bullet in nobody unless you got to. I want that privilege for me and my lil' homie." He opened the backdoor and waved at Quik and his men. They filed in right after one another.

I twisted the silencer into my DSK until it wouldn't spin no more. Once it was good and tight, I got ready to rush into the backdoor. I wasn't about to let Hood Rich kill no kids. I didn't give a fuck what he was on out there in Philly. Them women and those kids weren't about to lose their lives for nothing.

"Let's get it, bruh." He rushed into the backdoor leading into a kitchen.

There were pots bubbling on every eye on the stove. I turned them off and made my way into the living room where Quik and his men had everybody laid out on their stomachs with their hands on the backs of their heads. Quik threw three women onto their ass roughly after kicking in the bathroom door. They fell right next to the men with tears in their eyes. Then, one of his men brought the children that were upstairs and threw them on the floor too. They were crying and screaming at the top of their lungs. Seeing that weighed heavy on my heart. Hood Rich grabbed a dark-skinned, super heavy-set dude from the floor by his dreads, and slung him against the wall.

He put his DSK into his forehead and turned it sideways. "Bitch nigga, call yo' boy Kilroy right now and put him on speaker phone." He demanded.

I felt like Hood Rich was gon' whack that nigga's head off. I couldn't let them shortits see that. It would fuck them up for the rest of their lives. I couldn't have that on my conscious. One of the lil' girls looked to be the same age as Jahliya.

"Look, all of the women and all of the kids, y'all get up, now!" I ordered and started to pull them up one by one. They were crying louder and begging me not to kill them. They got into a huddle and hugged each other in total fear of their lives. "Everybody shut the fuck up! Now! Get in the bathroom or I will kill you. Let's go! Move it! Move it!" I hollered, pushing them just enough to get my point across.

They followed my directive boo-hooing. Tears ran down their faces. They looked so vulnerable. I got to thinking about my mother, Princess, Blaze, our unborn children, and Jahliya. Out of all of the things that I had done in my life, who was to say that something like that couldn't ever happen to them?

Once we stepped into the bathroom, they began to cry harder. The bathroom was extremely cramped with roaches crawling all over the walls. There was also one on the mirror. The little girl that had to be about Jahliya's age held on to the twelve-year-old's legs and cried until her little face was bright red. I felt sick to my stomach. I wanted to pick her up and console her.

"Look, y'all stay in here and nothing is going to happen to either one of you. I assure you that.

Keep this door closed until you no longer hear any commotion out there. Do I make myself clear?"

They nodded in unison. Before I closed the bathroom door, I patted down a few of the women and recovered a cell phone from Boscoe's baby's mother.

Hood Rich sat Boscoe's phone on the table so Kilroy could see him clearly. He held Boscoe by the throat. "Listen up, Kilroy, those Diamond Projects belong to me. I'm giving you your official thirty-day notice right now. I want you off my property before the end of next month, or heads gon' keep on rolling like this."

Boscoe made a move to knock Hood Rich's hand away, but it was too late. Hood Rich had pulled the trigger and spat three bullets into his forehead. The DSK jumped in his hand, then sent smoke to the ceiling. Boscoe shook on his feet. Blood spat out of the back of his head before a pool of plasma formed around his body on the floor.

Kilroy smiled into the phone and shook his head. "You fucking with the wrong nigga, Hood Rich. You gon' find that out in short time." The phone went dead.

Hood Rich stood in silence for what seemed like two whole minutes. "Kill everybody in this bitch. I don't want a single soul breathing when we leave this bitch. That's an order!" He hollered, standing over another man and putting two in the back of his head.

After hearing that, the other hostages started to panic and were gunned down and left within a pool of their own blood.

97

We were on our way out of the house through the backdoor when Quik stopped outside of the bathroom door and kicked it open. He took a step back after slamming a fresh magazine into his DSK and cocked it. I could hear the girls screaming.

"Nooo!" I hollered, running over to him. "Not them!"

He squeezed his trigger again with fire spitting from the barrel. His shells dropped onto the hallway floor. Two of the women staggered out of the bathroom with holes all over them. They fell to their face. Quik's shooter stepped up and finished them off. More shots were fired into the bathroom. More screaming from the girls. I rushed over and bumped Quik out of the way.

He flew into the wall, then regained his balance. "What the fuck you doing?" He hollered.

I raised my DSK and let lose six shots into his face, nearly knocking his head off. I turned to his shooter and hit him twice in the back. He fell on one of the women that were in the kitchen.

Quik's other two shooters had gone out of the backdoor already. They didn't have a clue what was going on inside. I made my way to the bathroom door and looked inside. The scene was enough to drive me instantly mad. Quik had massacred every female that had been in there. They were slumped over each other. Blood poured from their many gunshot wounds. Not a single one could have survived his assault. I swallowed and said a silent prayer in my head for their souls.

Hood Rich came up behind me and laid his hand on my shoulder. I shrugged it off and made my way outside. Quik's shooters were already in the van waiting for him. I walked right up to it, slid the side door back, and got in.

"What's taking kid 'n 'em so long, Dunn?" the driver asked me.

"Yeah, we gotta be out before Philly's fines show up to this bitch," said the passenger.

I raised the DSK and popped the driver twice in the head, and the passenger twice. Their blood splashed across the windshield.

I got out of the van and slammed the side door back. Then, I got in the Porsche and mugged Hood Rich. "Let's go, bruh. I'm ready to go back to Miami." I said, still seeing the picture of the female's slain bodies in my mind's eye.

***

Back at the hotel, Hood Rich poured three grams of cocaine on the lamp table and made four thick lines. He rolled a hundred-dollar bill and looked up at me "Taurus, you gotta let that shit go, lil' homie. Bitches gon' get killed from time to time. When I saw you move them hoes into the bathroom I knew you was trying save 'em. I didn't know that fool was gone do what he did."

I was pacing, heated. "Nigga if I ain't have the amount of respect for you that I did, I'd come over there and buss you in yo' shit. On everything." I flared my nostrils and mugged that nigga even harder. More flashes of the female's dead bodies popped into my head. It was getting me more and more heated.

Hood Rich stood up and his vest. "That's gon' allow you to get past this shit so we ca move forward with this mission? Huh?" He leaned over, snorted two lines, and pulled on his nose. He stood back up and held his arms out like a lower-cased T. "Come on, Taurus. Take yo' best shot. Get out yo' frustration."

I stopped in place and lowered my eyes. "Nigga, don't tempt me. One of them lil' girls in there was the same age as my daughter. She was a fucking baby! So, don't tempt me, Hood Rich."

Hood Rich threw his pistols on to the bed and frowned. "Nigga I don't give a fuck about none of them lil' bitches. This shit is all about supremacy and them lil' hoes was causalities of war, so suck that shit up and quit acting like a bitch."

I cocked my fist back and bussed him in the mouth so hard that he fell onto the bed, holding it as blood ran through his fingers. "Get up, nigga. Let me show you what these hands about."

Hood Rich jumped up with blood dripping off his chin. He jogged around the bed and swung with all his might. I ducked that blow and caught him with a right hook, left cross, then an uppercut that knocked his ass back on the bed. He picked up one of the pistols, and cocked it back, mugging me.

I took the .40 off of my hip' and cocked it. "Nigga, I'm letting you know that if you up that pistol on me you gon' have to kill me. I live by the same laws that you do."

He stood up, keeping the gun at his side. "Taurus, you my lil' nigga, bruh. We ain't finna fallout over this bullshit. I need yo' ass! Damn!" His chest heaved. Blood continued to drip from his chin.

"Them was females, bruh. Two of them were kids. Wasn't nothing bullshit about it. They ain't have nothing to do with Kilroy. Nothing!" I lowered my head and felt my heart pounding in my chest.

"Fuck you want me to do Taurus? I ain't pull the trigger. The nigga who did, you filled him up with shots. Him and his crew. So, what more do you want me to do? I even hit one of them for you. I wish I could change shit, but I can't, bruh. What's done is done. We gotta move on."

I shook my head. "I ain't feeling this Philly scene, Hood Rich. I gotta clear my head, dawg. I need some time away. You do what you gotta do to pick up these pieces, then, when you ready to close the deal out here I'll be by your side. But not right now. I'm out first thing it the morning."

Hood Rich held his chin and nodded. "That's understandable, lil' bruh. You take a few weeks and I'll get shit in order. In the meantime, I wanna show you some shit that will help you to understand what I'm trying to do. But we'll do that after you get your mind right. It's all love."

I didn't give a fuck what that nigga was talking about. I wanted to get back to Miami so I could make sure that my people were okay. I needed to hold Jahliya in my arms. "That's a bet bruh."

Chapter 8

It was three days later, and I was sitting on the side of the on the steps of our big swimming pool out back while I bounced Jahliya in the water. She had those pink floaties on her arms. Her long, curly hair was matted to her scalp. It was over ninety degrees outside with very little wind. The humidity wasn't that bad, but I was still hot.

I picked her up in the air and brought her down while she laughed and kicked her leg. I kissed her on her cheeks and dunked her into the water deep enough that it came to her stomach before hoisting her back in the air.

Blaze walked out of the mansion in a two-piece pink Prada bathing suit. Her stomach was poking out in front of her. She came over and sat beside me with a big smile on her face. She kissed my cheek, then turned my head so she could kiss me full on the lips, sucking on them for a short time, then rubbing her nose against mine. "Mmm, I missed you so much, baby."

"I missed you too."

Jahliyah splashed loudly in the pool in front of us.

"I missed you too, in there, baby girl." I leaned over and kissed Blaze's stomach, rubbing the side of my face against it.

She smacked my shoulder. "Ain't no girl in there."

I frowned. "Yes, it is. I can tell by how you're carrying. You just want it to be a boy," I teased. We decided not to have the sex of the baby revealed to us. The gender really didn't bother me one bit, but I could tell that Blaze really wanted a lil' boy. Every time she referred to our child, she always did so by using male pronouns.

She sighed. "Yeah, you might be right. We'll find out in a matter of months. Twelve weeks to go. Can't wait. I feel like I'm about to blow already." She blew air out of her jaws. Her face had gotten a little fatter since she had been pregnant.

It looked good to me though. I thought she was still a dime, and I was very picky to give a ten out to any female, whether she was mine or another man's. "I love you, boo."

"I love you too, sweetie." She smiled and closed her eyes. "So, while you were gone, I was able to do a little bonding with your mother, and I found out some very interesting things about you."

"Is that right?" I allowed Jahliya to swim around a little bit. Whenever she had gotten away, I'd pull her back to me. Her deep dimples were prominent on each cheek as she laughed.

"Yeah, that's right. I found out the reason she named you Taurus. It's because it's your sign. You were born on April the twenty-seventh in Cook County Hospital in Chicago, Illinois. You were seven pounds and eleven ounces. She also told me that growing up, your favorite food was pizza, and second to that is Gyros. Is that still the same to this day?" he put her hand over her forehead to block the rays from the sun.

I squirted a fifty cent-sized bit of suntan lotion into the palm of my hand and rubbed it all over her stomach. "Yep, that ain't ever gon' change."

She laughed. "That's crazy, because that's my favorite food in the exact same order. I guess it'll be our son's, too."

I laughed at her and sat Jahliya on my thigh. "That will be crazy."

Princess walked into the backyard with red G string all up in her ass. Her cheeks jiggled as she walked past. I'd also noted that both nipples were poking through her red bikini top. She looked good enough to eat. She sat on the other end of the pool with her knees to her chest. Her crotch band did very little to hide her bald pussy lips. I felt my piece rising.

Blaze sucked her teeth. "I know that girl know she showing you her pussy right now. I want a say something to her so bad, but I don't feel like arguing. Ugh, she so annoying." Blaze sat closer to me, laid her head on my shoulder, then kissed my cheek. "I love you, Taurus. With all of my heart. Do you hear me?"

I nodded and watched Princess run her hand up and down her inner thigh. She licked her juicy lips and adjusted her Chanel sunglasses on her face. I was imagining what her pussy felt like. I wanted some of that gushy. It had been a minute. "I love you too, boo. For the rest of my life."

She grabbed my chin and turned it, so I could look into her pretty brown eyes. Are you saying that to me or her right now?" She rolled her eyes, stood up and walked into the house. I wanted to stop her, but Princess had my focus.

Less than a minute later, I was sitting beside Princess' lil' sexy ass, eyeing her body down with hunger. I handed Jahliya to her. "Here, hold her for a minute."

She giggled. "What's the matter? Looks like you got trouble in paradise. She kissed Jahliya's cheeks and blew into her face. She smelled like Gucci perfume and her hair was micro braided. It flowed to the top of her shoulders. She had pink diamond earrings in her ears that matched her sunglasses. Her nails were stamped with a Gucci logo, as were her toes. I was sitting there feening for her worse than ever.

"Nah, it's good. She just needed to get away from the heat for a minute, I guess. What's good with you, though?"

She bounced Jahliya in the water in front of her. "I'm good. I'm going out later on tonight to shake my groove thang for a lil' bit. I got one of my friends flying from Jersey. He just got out from doing a nickel upstate." She licked her lips.

"Don't play with me, shawty. No nigga bet not be flyin' in from nowhere. Especially if he think he coming to my crib. I'll knocked that nigga's head off and make you burry his ass in the backyard. Don't get shit twisted.

"Ooh, daddy, you said a bad word," Jahliya chimed in.

I took her out of Princess' hands and placed her in the big playpen we'd gotten for her that had a security gate around it. I took the floaties off her arms, and she ran and jumped on her Big Wheel. I locked the gate in place and sat beside Princess again. "You got a nigga comin' down here for real?"

She ran her finger along the crease between her thigh and her mound. She pulled her band aside just enough for me to see her slit, then popped it back in place. "I need some dick. He been down for a minute. I know he ain't gon' play with this pussy. Besides, what you about it for? You and Blaze had to fuck before you left to go with Hood Rich. You good." Her hand landed back between her legs She pulled on her sex lips, then slid her fingers deep inside herself, moaning. "I'm so wet. I gotta get this beat in. I can't take this no more. I gotta call his ass." She stood up and dusted her ass cheeks off. She had completely swallowed the bikini bottom with her cheeks.

"Princess, don't play with me. I been giving you a lot of leeway, but I ain't finna take some other nigga walkin' around my pad. You ain't gon' do shit but get homeboy ass killed. Keep acting like you don't know what it is."

"Aww, look at you putting stipulations on what I can do while I'm living under this roof." She frowned. "Nigga this is my house too. You ain't finna be the only on up in here fucking. What's good for the goose is good for the gander. Now I said that I'm bringin' a friend. I need this cat hit. If I can stay away from killing that bitch, even though I know what you and her been on ever since we got here, then you can let me do me. I'm not fuckin' with you no more anyway. I can do better." She curled her upper lip and bumped me as she walked past.

I got to having all types of visions of choking her ass out, literally, until the breath left her body. I couldn't imagine no other nigga between her legs, making her moan and all of that. That image got me so sick that I could barely breathe. Now why was it that men could go off and fuck another female, even if they were in love, and it would mean nothing to them? But if the female they loved did the same thing it made them want to beat the shit out of her and kill the nigga that had just climbed from between her legs? I was one of those types. I wanted to keep doing my thing with Blaze, but I didn't want Princess fucking off with another dude. I wasn't gon' stand for that. I wished we could've all slept and fucked in the same bed as a happy family. That would have made me the happiest man.

***

Princess stayed out late that night. For some reason I couldn't sleep. I was kind of worried about her. I found myself at three in the morning downstairs in the big kitchen pouring myself a glass of orange juice.

My mother walked into the kitchen, rubbing her eyes. She had on a short blue and black negligee that stopped just below her mound. Her thick thighs shook with each step that she took. I could tell that she wasn't wearing a bra because her thick nipples were pressed against the silk material and I could make out the brown of them. "That girl still ain't home yet?" She stepped up to me and kissed my lips, wrapping her arms around my body, hugging me tightly.

I ran my fingers through her curly hair that stopped just below her waist, all natural. She popped back on her legs and looked up at me.

"N'all, she ain't came in yet. She ain't answering my texts either. I don't know what's good." I tried to not think the worst. I hoped she was just out being Princess. A pain in my fucking side.

My mother ran her right hand over my stomach muscles and bit into her bottom lip. "Is Blaze sleep?" She rubbed my chest with both hands, looking into my eyes real seductive like.

I nodded. "Yeah, she just fell out about an hour ago. When I left the room, she was snoring a lil' bit." I laughed at that.

She reached in between my legs and grabbed a hold of my penis, squeezing it in her hand before sliding it into my pajamas, taking hold of it. "Taurus. It's been a while, and I need some. Seriously." She kissed my chest and licked around my left nipple while she pumped my dick. "Can I have some?"

Damn I hated when she put me in that position. It was something about my mother that just rove me insane. Every time she came at me I wanted to say no. Just then, when I looked her up and down from head to toe, she was so damn bad to me. Not to mention, it was forbidden.

The scent of her caused me to feel some type of way. On top of that, my mother was strapped. Forty plus years old and had the body of a top-notch stripper. She was high a yellow Creole, mixed with Black and Indian. Her eyes were hazel and sometimes flipped to straight green. She had real cute freckles along her nose and a mole on her upper lip on the left side. She stayed well-groomed from head to toe, and as crazy as it was, her sex game was incredible to me. She had that vet pussy. So, she knew how to work them walls and do all of the things that drove me crazy. I called her my addiction.

Somehow, someway, we made it upstairs, all the way up to the third level in one of the guest rooms. I kicked the door closed, and before it slammed, she was kissing all over my neck, stroking my penis.

"I want some of this, baby. Mama need you. I need you so bad." She bit at my neck with vigor.

I reached around and rubbed all over that fat ass booty, squeezing it. I had the negligee around lower waist. My hand slipped between her cheeks and rubbed over her kitty. I slipped two fingers into her and fucked them in and out at full speed. She bit my chest.

"Unn! Yes, baby! Get it for me. Please, mommy."

She forced my pajama bottoms down my thighs, dropped her knees and quickly stroked my pipe. "I gotta taste my baby. I gotta taste you, honey." She kissed my head and licked around it. She then sucked me into her mouth, spearing her head into my lap.

My eyes rolled into the back of my head as I grabbed a handful of her curly hair and guided her back and forth, even though I didn't need to. She was a vet by all means. "Damn, ma!" I groaned and humped into her mouth. She was making slurping sounds that drove me crazy.

She popped me out of her mouth and smiled up at me. "Those girls can't do you like mama can. Can they, baby?" She pulled me into her mouth again and placed her hands on my thighs, sucking me at full speed. "Cum for me, Taurus. Cum for mama."

I moaned and made all kinds of noises while she tamed me. My toes curled, and I knew I couldn't hold back any longer. Her scent wafted up my nose and it was over. I came so hard that I fell against her. She pushed me back against the wall and kept milking me for all I was worth. Then she sucked me until I was rock hard.

She stood up, shimmying her negligee up her wide hips. Her pussy had a nice amount of hair on it, though it wasn't a big bush. It didn't prevent me from seeing them thick sex lips. She laid on the bed and opened her thick thighs wide. Afterward, she opened her pussy lips for me. "Your turn. Come on, babe. Mama need you." She moaned and pinched her left nipple. Her supple breast bounced.

I sucked all over her right thigh and licked it before doing the same thing to the other one. She was so thick.

She grabbed my head and guided me to her center. "We ain't got that long. I need you right there." She arched her back.

I sucked both lips into my mouth, pulling them apart. I slid my tongue deep within her womb, stabbing it while I pinched her clit.

She shivered. "Unn! Yes, baby! Just like that. Do mama right."

I folded her lips all the way back, trapped her clit with my lips and sucked on it hard while her juices oozed down my throat. She tasted like salt and sugar at the same time. The taste was forbidden yet alluring. The more I swallowed, the more I craved her juices.

She wrapped her thighs around my face and started to ride it fast and hard. "Yes! Yes. Yes, baby. My baby! You gon' make me. You gon' make me. Ooh, yes!" She started to shiver like crazy. She threw her head back and groaned within throat before pushing me away from her. "Aww, fuck!" She ran her fingers up and down her slit, sliding them in and out of her center. "Give me some, right now! Hurry, baby!" She laid back and opened her thick thighs wife.

I climbed right between them and slid all the way in, slamming hard. She moaned in my ear and wrapped her legs around my waist, rubbing my back. My dick thrusted in and out of her at full speed. Globs of her juices poured out of her, dripping down her ass cheek. I wrapped my arms around her neck and rocked up and down, long-stroking her and kissing all over her lips. Her forbidden pussy sucked at me.

"Un. Un. Un, mama. Damn. It's. So. Good." I gasped, enjoying her.

"Yes. Yes. Son. Harder. You love your mama, don't you?" she whispered, enticing me. She humped into, begging me to go deeper.

I ain't have a problem doing it. I flipped her on all fours, pounding her from the back. She looked over her shoulder at me. Her titties swung on her chest with her nipples heavily engorged. I rubbed all over that clit until she came on my pipe, shaking like crazy.

"Un! Fuck! Like. That."

She fell onto her stomach and I kept on hittin' that cat like my life was on the line, howling the whole time.

She reached around herself and rubbed all over my lower back and ass while I continued to long-stroke that pussy. "Taurus, my ass, baby. Do my ass, baby. Hurry up." She gasped.

I allowed her to rise to her knees, bent her all the way over with her face in the bed and slowly slid into her backdoor.

"Uuh! Baby! Aww! Wait a minute! She whimpered, holding her cheeks apart.

"This it, mama! No. More. You. Hear. Me." I said, sliding in and out of her backdoor.

She whimpered underneath me, squeezing her cheeks together.

"Yes. Okay. Okay. I. Hear you. I hear you. Baby." She slammed back into me and beat her fist on the bed with her eyes closed.

I'd taken a hold of her clit, pinching it, and running my thumb in circles around it. I couldn't have been in that ass for more than fifteen minutes before my body was tensing up. I got the shivers. I felt my orgasm coming from all over me. My eyes rolled into the back of my head. I couldn't take it no more. "It's coming, Mama. It's coming." I fucked faster and faster, as my seed spilled out of me. I noticed her going crazy on her clitoris. As I was coming, she was as well. We collapsed in the bed, breathing hard, and smelling like straight sex.

***

After the shower, I pulled her back into the same room and hugged her to my body. "Look,

Mama. I love you with all of my heart, but on my daughter and my unborn child, that will never happen again. It can't." I held the side of her face.

She nodded and blinked tears. "I know, baby. I just wat you to know that I love you just as much as you love me. You're the only male in this world that I've ever felt any love from, and I don't regret any of the things that we have done together. They were needed, regardless of what the world may say about it." She blinked, and tears slid down her face. She placed her hand on my chest. "Your mother is supposed to be dead right now, son. Had it not been for you, I would have been gone a Long, long time ago. But you kept me here. You protected me. You loved me. You saved me. I am grateful." She kissed my lips and took a deep breath. "Ma, got to go now. I gotta go my own way. I've been lost and misled ever since I was fourteen years old and your father took me away from my family." She shook her head. "But it's time, baby. We'll never do this again. I promise." She stepped on her tippy toes and hugged me tightly. I could hear her sobbing into my ear. Her body shook.

I felt that she was literally releasing me. We had been through so much as mother and son. Against all odds I had always been that one that she could depend on to save her, and I always would be, regardless of if we ever laid down together again. She was my queen by any means. I kissed her forehead and wiped her tears with my thumbs, looking into her beautiful eyes and face. "I love you ma. I don't regret nothing that we've ever done, so never feel that you've hurt me in any way. You will forever be my heart and soul, and I'm thankful for you." I hugged her back to me, and we stood there for the next five minutes embraced.

True to our words, that was the last time that me and my mother had ever gotten down. I have never regretted any of the times that we had. I never will. I felt that we had one of those relationships that was all our own. It was needed, and it'd gotten the both of us through some extremely tough times in life when all we had was each other.

Chapter 9

Two weeks later, after me and Blaze came from the grocery store picking up a few items, we pulled into the driveway to find Princess and some dark-skinned, husky nigga embraced in front of the mansion. I wouldn't find out until a bit later that the nigga's name was Silas. He was 6-feet tall and bald-headed with tattoos all over his neck and arms. His mouth was full of gold and he wore glasses.

As I pulled my Benz into the driveway, I saw that she kissed his lips. He grabbed her ass. The whole time Jahliya played on her tricycle, not more than three yards away from them. That got me more pissed than anything. Before I even put the car in park, I'd grabbed my .40 Glock and placed it on my lap.

Blaze grabbed my wrist. "Baby, please don't get out here and do nothin' stupid. You know all that girl is doing is trying to get a rise out of you. She's testing your gangsta. Don't let her play you like that. Please." She begged, turning my face so that I looked into her brown eyes instead of the display of affection that Princess put on in the front of the mansion.

I had visions of walking up to Silas and putting two in his face. I ain't want no nigga feeling all over my baby mother like that. I was a pure hater. Since Jahliya came out of the pussy I felt like her womb belonged to me from then on. It took every ounce of will power that I had in me to not jump out and get on some straight bullshit.

Blaze kissed my cheek. "Babe, I bet if you don't play into her lil' game, just walk right past her with your arm around my neck, it's going to make her sick. Watch what she does. The only way to win this type of war she's playing is to show her that we're happy. Trust me. There is no bigger blow to a female's gut than to know you're happy."

I looked into her eyes as my anger subsided and nodded. "A'ight, boo, I'ma take your lead. I'm just letting you know that shit gon' be it for me. You know I hate niggas. Then there is Jahliya to think about. I don't want no an around her if it ain't me, period."

She rubbed the side of my "Calm down, baby. I know. I understand how you are, and I get it. But this is just the games that baby mother's play. I won't, 'cuz I know yo' ass crazy. But clearly, she don't care about that. It gets better. Let's get these groceries in the house."

There were only three bags. I grabbed all three of the, then walked around and opened Blaze's door for her, placing my arm around her shoulders. I kissed her on the cheek as we made our way to the front of the mansion where Silas and Princess were still in their embrace.

As we made it to the top of the stairs, Princess kiss lips one more time, and turned to us with a smile on her face. "Oh, I'm sorry. Taurus, Blaze, this is my man, Silas. He's from New Jersey. We used to go to high school together."

I smiled and nodded. "Yeah, what it do, bruh? How you loving this Miami weather?" I asked, imagining emptying a clip into his face. I would reload and empty it all over again a until he was unrecognizable for is funeral. They'd have to put a black over his face for when viewers walked by to view him in his casket.

He extended his hand. "It's good, Kid. It feel odd being out of Jersey, but my shorty begged me to come down and fuck with her. How could I say no?" He pulled Princess into him and kissed her lips.

I felt my blood boiling. Blaze must've felt it too because she held me tighter and rubbed my chest. I was seconds away from smoking this stud. I looked over to Jahliya, and she was busy blowing bubbles. I was thankful for that. I didn't want her to see her mother behaving like that with some other dude, though I guess it was a bit of a double standard because me and Blaze stayed hugged up in front of her.

I brushed his hand to the side. I could only fake the funk so much. I wasn't about to shake his hand. "Say, I don't know what it is with you two, but all I ask is that y'all don't be doing all that in front of my daughter. Let's keep them curse words to a minimum too. That's all I ask."

Princess wiped her lips and looked into my eyes, lowering hers before she smiled. "I got this. We'll be good in front of her. Ain't that right baby?" She looked up to Silas and kissed his lips again with her eyes closed.

He nodded then broke the embrace. "I can respect that. She is a female. That make sense." He extended his hand toward me.

I shook my head. "It ain't that type of party, nigga." I turned to Princess. "I don't care what you do, but this nigga ain't coming into my crib. So y'all 1 figure it out." I wrapped my arm around Blaze's shoulder and walked past them on our way into the house.

Princess jogged around and got into my face. "Hold on, Taurus, 'cuz that was rude as hell. Me and you already talked about this. I thought we had an understanding."

I looked down at her and once again tried to keep my cool. "What understanding was that, Princess?"

"You said that this is just as much my house as it is ours. That I can do me. Well, I'm doing me, and you're doing you, so what's the problem?" She flared her nostrils.

It had to be about ninety degrees outside. There wasn't any wind blowing, and it was even humid this day. I was hot and already irritated. I ain't like beefing with her. "Shawty, I don't care about you doing you. You just ain't finna bring no nigga into this crib. I don't care who they is. I don't even let the gardeners come inside. I don't know that nigga, and even if I did, it ain't happening. He's more welcome to chill in the pool house though. Just not the mansion."

Silas stepped up and waved his hand. "It's good. I can stay in a Telly, Princess. I ain't gotta be in Kid's crib if he don't want me to."

Princess shook her head. "N'all, fuck that. This my crib too. I say you staying. That's gon' be that. Taurus just need to get off of that bullshit. I ain't fuckin' with you and Blaze, so y'all don't fuck with me." She snapped. "I ain't forgot what she did to me,

Taurus. You bet not forget either. That's all I'm saying." She mugged Blaze with an evil scowl on her face.

Blaze squeezed my hand and looked up at me. "Baby, just let this matter go. It's not that serious."

I was so heated that sweat was pouring down the side of my face. My trigger finger was itching real bad. "A'ight. You know what? It's good. I'ma let y'all do y'all. Just keep them words clean in front of my daughter. If y'all finna get on anything physical, Princess, take her to my mother's room. If I'm here, bring her to me. Other than that, it's good."

She curled her lip and nodded. "Yeah, it better be. Come on, Silas. Jahliya! Jahliya! Come on, baby, it's time to go inside the house." She yelled to our daughter.

***

That night, me and Blaze ordered Meat Lover's pizza and hugged up in front of the big projector and watched the movie *Love Me When It Hurts.* She sat in front of me while I wrapped my arms around her and kissed her neck. I'd feed her a bite of pizza at a time then hold her drink for her. I was treating her like a queen, and she was loving every minute of it.

Halfway through the movie she laid on my chest and sighed. "Taurus, you still in love with Princess, ain't you?"

I held her for a minute and watched the movie play a lil' while without answering her question. It had caught me off guard. "Yeah, I guess I am. Why you ask me that?"

She shrugged. "I guess I just wanted to see if you were going to tell me the truth." She exhaled. "I saw that possessive look in your eye today, and I can't lie and say that it didn't hurt me because it did. I never saw that look for me in them, so I guess my next question is, if you love her so much, why are you here with me? Why haven't you flat out chosen her and y'all just live your lives together? To be honest, I'm tired of being in the middle. I'm tired of sharing your heart." She grabbed the remote, so she could pause the movie and straddle me.

I looked into her eyes for a long time without words. "Blaze, I know I'm supposed to be with you. I think I been knowin' that ever since the first week we spent together. That was the first time I truly felt happy with a female. You made everything fun. I was able to be a kid with you, and during those days we shared, I forgot about the slums. That's something I've never been able to do.

She rubbed her cheek against mine and said, "I love you and you me, Taurus. Do you ever fear losing me to someone else?" Her eyes got watery as she searched mine.

I nodded. "Blaze, I love you with all my heart. I could never recover if I lost you. Ever since you've been in my life, you've made it all about me. You been so one hunnit, and you deserve so much better. I'm starting to see that."

Tears rolled down her cheeks heavily. "Then give it to me, Taurus. Give me that man that I deserve. You already know that I am all for you. I would never do any of the things that she's doing to you. I just want us to have a strong family. I want you and I love you with all my heart. We shouldn't be able to be penetrated. It's not fair. If you don't see the same thing, then you have to release me. You have to let me go so I can find what I need. I am begging you to." She cried and beat her fist on my shoulder with her face in my chest.

I rubbed her back and closed my eyes. I felt horrible. Anytime Blaze cried and I was the reason, it made me feel like the worst man in the world. I knew that she genuinely loved me and that she wanted the best for not only me but us as a whole. She didn't deserve any of the things I put her through. I had to do better for us.

I picked up her face and kissed her lips even though snot had dripped onto them. I didn't care. I wiped her tears away and held my face against her which I held in my hands. "I'm choosin' you, Blaze. I know I done messed up a whole lot since we've been together, and I still don't have everything figured out. But I love you, and you're who I want to be with for the rest of my life. I gotta be a man and be the best that I can be to you and our child, even before he or she gets here."

She sniffed, and I wiped more of her tears away. "So, what does that mean? And I need you to be honest with me. I can't take these games anymore."

"It means that I want you to be my wife. I wanna settle down with you faithfully after we tie that knot. That's if you're willing to be my wife against all odds."

She looked into my eyes. "Baby, I know it's not that easy. Even if you're telling me that you want me to be your wife, it can't happen like that, even if we wanted it to. Princess is a problem. Your life style is a problem. Your sex drive and lust for other women is a problem. How could I ever make a marriage work with all of the variables against us?"

I lowered my head. "I guess we'll take it one day at a time. It's for me to set the standard and have everything in order before our child get here. I wanna walk you down that aisle and allow for this baby to come into the world while we are bound in holy matrimony. I know that."

Her eyes searched through mine intently. I could tell that she was trying her best to see into my soul. She wanted so desperately to believe in my words. Meanwhile, I was going through my own mental battle. I honestly loved Blaze like crazy, and between the two, Princess was more like me. She was hood, raw, rugged and believed in an eye for an eye. I couldn't see us lasting before one of us killed the other. I couldn't do her like that or keep putting my hands on her. My mother always told me that if a man felt the need to put his hands on a woman, then he needed to leave her alone. It was as simple as that.

My love for Princess had become a form of possession than actual bliss. I wasn't happy with her. Our past kept me bonded to her more than anything. The only time I felt any true sense of happiness or peace was when I was with Blaze.

"Baby, if you just give me a chance, I can show you how truly serious I am."

She shook her head and sat back on her haunches. "Damn, Taurus, I don't know how you got me so gone in the head, but I'm out of bounds, baby. I love you so much and I'm going to give you the chance that you're asking for. Just, please, don't hurt me. I can't take any more pain." She wrapped her arms around my neck. I held onto her for the rest of the night.

***

At two in the morning, Princess knocked on the bedroom door and stepped inside, holding a sleeping Jahliya in her arms. "Psst! Taurus, come get this girl. We about to get our groove on and I don't want her waking up in the middle of it." She handed Jahliya to me and slowly walked away with her red boy shorts all up in the crack of her ass. Her every step caused her cheeks to jiggle.

I laid Jahliya in bed. I couldn't do nothing but shake my head.

Chapter 10

A month later, I helped Blaze into her seat, along with the Maître D. She scooted her chair forward and handed her a menu that didn't have any prices on it. We were seated at one of the beach's finest five-star restaurants called Poppy's. It had a red carpet all the way through it. It took me a month just to get on the list, and even then, they tried to cancel my damn reservation twice until Hood Rich made a call to the Cuban drug lord that owned the restaurants.

Blaze was eight months pregnant and technically wasn't supposed to be out of the house or the bed. Her obstetrician had told us three times that she was in jeopardy of dying or losing our child early. Even though I was worried about that, there was something that I just needed to do.

The restaurant was dimly-lit. The sounds of crystal glasses and china could be heard being used at nearly every table. The music was soft and soothing. Each table was evenly spaced from the other. The majority of the patrons were those that were rich and famous.

The Maître D poured lemonade into Blaze's glass and set the pitcher on the table and walked away.

Blaze took a deep breath and put her right hand on her big stomach. "Taurus, it feels good to be out of that mansion. Lord knows I can barely breathe. We gon' have to get up out of here." She took a sip of her lemonade.

I laughed at her and grabbed her hand. "Barely. I was trying to be a lil' romantic. I guess I dropped the ball on that."

She shook her head and smiled. "N'all, Poppy's is an act of trying to be very romantic for a day. I'm flattered and stuffed with this turkey you put inside of me," she joked. She then inhaled and exhaled slowly.

I laughed again. I had to get my baby back to the crib. "A'ight. Well, without further ado." I got up and helped her out of her chair. Then, I took the Pristine Jewelers jewelry box out of my pocket that held her three carat diamond engagement ring inside of it. I stepped closer to her and dropped to one knee.

She held her hand over her mouth and her eyes had gotten buck. She started to fan her eyes, shaking her head.

"Blaze, I know I'm not perfect and I'm out here in these streets. I got a shady past and my baby mother is more than a seven-forty-seven can carry, but I love you. I been loving you ever since I was nineteen years old. You were the first person that taught me how to think beyond the ghetto. You're carrying my seed. I'm crazy about you and I wanna make it official." I kissed her left hand and continued to hold it. "Will you be my wife? Give me the chance to be the man that I know I can be for you? Because I need you and I can't live my life without you."

Tears slid down her cheeks. "Taurus, if you promise that you'll love me unconditionally with all of your heart and loyalty, I'll marry you. I'll marry you and be the best wife to you that you'd ever think of." She spread her fingers in anticipation.

I slid the ring onto her finger before helping her up, so I could hug her lil' body.

***

That same night, my mother and Blaze hugged each other in the kitchen while my mother admired her ring. "Damn, son, you must really love this girl. Her rock is as big as a mountain."

Blaze sucked her teeth. "I'm in love with him, I deserve it. It should be bigger than this. But this is only the beginning. Ain't that right, babe?" She leaned forward and kissed my lips.

"You already know."

Princess came down the stairs with Jahliya in her arms and a frown on her face. "Why y'all down here makin' all this damn noise? We're up there trying to sleep." she snapped.

My mother bucked her eyes and held her hands at shoulder-length. "I don't even wanna be around for this. I'm letting y'all know now that I don't want y'all fightin' in here. We left that back in Texas. Do y'all understand me?" She asked, looking from Blaze to Princess.

Princess scrunched her eyebrows. "Ain't nobody finna be fightin', mama. Why would you say that?" she asked, handing Jahliya to my mother. Her eyes got bucked.

Blaze shook her head. "It's an engagement ring."

Princess looked up and mugged me. "An engagement ring from who, Blaze?"

Blaze slowly made her way off the stool, holding her back. She stepped behind me. "Taurus, you know I ain't in no position to fight that girl. You need to tell her what it is."

Princess clenched her teeth. "You're tryin' to marry this bitch?" She began to walk toward us with her small fists balled up.

I frowned. "Yeah, that's what I'ma do. It's time I quit playin' and make it official." I turned around and put my arm around Blaze, making sure that I was in a position to block her from Princess in case she did try and get on some bullshit.

Princess stood in place, staring daggers into the side of my head. "This is how you gon' do us, Taurus? You gon' marry this bitch and leave us out in the cold? Really?" She continued to stare me down as we walked out of the kitchen.

When we got to the bottom of the stairs, I could hear the silverware drawer open and slam loudly. She hollered and pulled a butcher's knife out of the cutter's set on the counter. She made her way in our direction.

I got Blaze to the top of the stairs before Princess got to the bottom with the knife in her hand. "Go in the room and close the door. Let me holler at her, okay?" I said, looking down the stairs at Princess.

Blaze nodded, took a deep breath, blew it out, and took in another. "Okay, baby."

Princess was on her way up the stairs, taking one step at a time. "Taurus, I'm finna kill you and that bitch! I swear to God! I can't believe you doin' this shit to me!"

Blaze held her lower back and waddled down the hallway toward the room. She stopped and screamed at the top of her lungs before her water broke. "Taurus, help me!"

Princess wiped her tears and began up the stairs again. "I'm finna kill you, Taurus."

I waited until she got to the stairs. She swung the knife, trying her best to lash me across the face. I jumped back and took a hold of her wrist. "I'm tired of goin' through this with you, Princess." I grabbed her by the throat, holding her against the wall.

"Taurus, let her go!" my mother yelled. "That's not right, baby!"

Jahliya screamed at the top of her lungs and jumped in my mother's arms. "Mommy! Stop, daddy! Stop!" she cried.

Blaze fell to her butt and scooted against the wall. "I need help. Please, someone call the ambulance. Uhhh!" She hollered, holding her stomach. She took deep breaths with her eyes wide open.

My mama put my daughter down and ran to her aid.

Jahliya rand over and grabbed my pant leg, pulling on it. "Let mommy down, daddy."

I banged Princess' wrist so she could drop the knife and kicked it down the stairs. Then, I picked her up and took her to the room, kicking the door closed. "What the fuck is wrong with you?" I hollered, blocking the doorway. I tossed her on the bed inside the guest room.

"What the fuck is wrong with me, Taurus? You proposed to that bitch! That's what the fuck is wrong with me!" She bounced off the bed and tried to get past me." Get out of my way, Taurus. I need to get my baby!" she snapped.

Jahliya beat on the door. "Mommy! Please! Mommy!" She was becoming hysterical.

I opened the door and snatched Jahliya up. "Baby, be quiet. She's okay." I pointed to Princess.

Jahliya wiggled in my arms until I put her on the floor. She ran to princess and jumped into her arms. "Mommy, are you okay?"

Princess sat back on the bed and rocked with Jahliya. "I'm okay, baby. We were playing a game. That's all." She mugged me again and nodded as if to say that this wasn't over.

I peeked out of the door and saw my mother giving Blaze two big pillows, placing a wet cloth over her forehead. I knew I needed to be out there so I could comfort her.

"Princess, I'm begging you, shawty. You tryin' to get me to do something to you that I never wanna do. All this shit is unhealthy. We gotta go our separate ways. I'm serious."

"This how you gon' do me, Taurus? Okay, I'ma let you have this. Gon' 'head. I hope y'all are happy together." She stood with Jahliya in her arms.

I looked out of the door again.

Blaze had pain written all over her face. She looked drained as if she was fighting to keep it all together. "Taurus! I need you, baby!"

"Gon' 'head, Taurus. Life is too short. I don't even care no more. I mean it this time."

"Princess, we just need to get an understanding, but right now ain't the time. I gotta get her to the hospital before she lose our kid."

"Go make sure your fiancée is good. I swear I ain't gon' do shit. I'm over this shit. That's my word." She sat back on the bed and rocked.

I couldn't really tell if she was going to be on bullshit or not, but I couldn't leave Blaze in that hallway down and out like she was. I had to get her to the hospital, and that's what I did.

It took me ten minutes to get her into my Navigator, and another thirty before we made it to the hospital where my mother ran inside and got two nurses to meet me at my truck. They sat Blaze in a wheel chair and rushed her back inside with her screaming at the top of her lungs, holding her stomach.

"Taurus! Taurus! I need you!"

My heart was pounding in my chest as I held her hand and jogged alongside the wheelchair. "Baby, you gon' be alright, I promise. I love you. Do you hear me?"

She wailed and squeezed her eyes tightly together. "Yes! I love you too, Taurus! I love you so much!" In one breath, she fainted. Her head fell into her lap.

I felt like I was going to pass out right there in that long hallway. "Blaze! Blaze! What just happened to her?" I hollered, panicking out of my mind.

"Sir, you can't go past this point! We're sorry. We'll take it from here," one of the nurses said, placing both of her hands on my chest to stop me from going any further.

"That's my fiancée. I have to be by her side." I tried to fight to get past her and would've succeeded had ten more nurses and a security guard to stop me.

My mother pulled my arm. "Taurus! It's okay, baby. Just let them do their job. Come with me."

I reluctantly allowed for her to guide me out of the hallway and into the waiting room where wound up staying for sixteen hours before one of the doctors came out and told us anything. By that time, my mother had to go and talk to him because I fear what I would've done to him. He pulled her to the side and spoke to her in the middle of the hallway while nurses jogged past them.

When all was said and done, my mother walked back over to me with a solemn look on her face. I had my head down, watching Sports Center on my phone. They were about to announce where LeBron was going to spend his sixteenth season in the league. I was hoping for Houston or even the Lakers.

My mother sat beside me and rubbed my back. "She's doing okay, baby. She's in labor now, and the doctor assured me that they have their best nurse taking good care of her."

I jumped. "Labor? Hell, n'all, mama! I should be in there. She is about to give birth to my child. Wait. It's early. Should I be worried?"

She pulled my arm. "Baby, no, you shouldn't. She's going to be okay, but they do have to be extra careful with her, since she is going into labor prematurely. He is going to allow you to be present. When you go in there, son, do not get in the way. Let the people do their job. Comfort her. Can you do that?" She asked looking up at me and waiting for the doctor to come over to us.

***

Ten minutes later, after washing my arms and hands, they threw blue scrubs on me, and a pair of covers over my shoes. Finally, they allowed me access to the delivery room with Blaze. I almost broke my neck trying to get over to her. She grabbed my hand as they worked on her lower half.

The doctor urged her to push, and that made her squeeze my hand tighter. Her face scrunched as she let out harsh breaths.

"Ttuuhh! Huhh! Awww!" She hollered with sweat pouring down the side of her face.

"It's okay. You got this, baby. I'm right here. I ain't going nowhere. I swear I love you so much. You hear me?" I kissed her forehead, and then her hand. I hated to see her in so much pain. I wished I could have taken the pain that she was feeling so that she wouldn't have had to.

"Yes, Taurus, I hear you. I hear you, baby. Awww! Shit!" Her breathing picked up, and she leaned forward, taking a hold of her knees. She pushed so hard that a vein appeared in the middle of her forehead. Then she fell back, still breathing heavily.

"Alright, I'm starting to see something here. I need you to push a little harder ma'am. Give it all that you have. Come on." The doctor encouraged from between her legs.

Blaze sat up and grabbed her knees. She huffed and puffed, closed her eyes and pushed. "Taurus!

Huh! Baby!" She hollered again, then started to strain.

I laid my face against the right side of hers. I tried to calm her. "I'm here, baby. We got this. We got this from here on out. Just us, Blaze. I appreciate you so much, baby. I promise I do."

Her breathing sped up and her chest heaved. Her jaws puffed inward and out. Thank you. Thank you! Awww-s! Ah!" She screamed, pushing once again.

"Okay, its crowning. Here it comes. Here it comes. Keep pushing, ma'am. You got this. You're almost there."

I wiped the sweat out of her eyes and she squeezed my hand so hard that it felt like my bones were being crushed into dust. I felt like hollering as loud as she was. Instead, I absorbed that pain and kept it encouraging her to get closer and closer to the finish line. "Come on, baby. We're almost there. Push for me. Push!" I held my face against hers until she brought our child into this world.

***

Our son was born prematurely at four pounds and ten ounces. As soon as he was delivered, the doctors rushed him to the emergency portion of the hospital. They were saying that he had an overwhelming amount of fluid in his lungs and they had to drain them as soon as possible.

I tried to follow behind them, but I was stopped by the medical staff and two security guards. They assured me that as long as they tended to him right away, he would be fine. I was secretly praying to God that they were telling me the truth. I couldn't stand to lose our child.

After Blaze gave birth, the nurses came and cleaned her. I kept on planting kisses all over her face. I loved and respected her so much. I felt like I owed this woman my life for bringing our child into the world. I immediately started to regret all the times I had hurt her or had taken her for granted.

Our son was in surgery for four hours and then placed in the Neonatal Intensive Care Unit where he was to stay for two straight weeks. After that, they moved him to another portion of the hospital for high-risk infants where he stayed for an additional week.

Slowly but surely, he had become stronger and bigger. When he'd gotten up to seven pounds, they removed his IVs and allowed for Blaze to feed him by breast. Three days after that, he was discharged as a healthy newborn at nine pounds and fifteen ounces. I was so thankful that I dropped to my knees and sent prayers up to the Man above.

Since he was born on August 23rd, we named him after that month and gave him Blaze's father's name, which was Ernest. My baby was so pale during his first two months that I gave him the nickname Ghost. Every time I called him by his nickname, his eyes would light up. He would smile and kick his little legs, so this name stuck for me and Blaze.

Chapter 11

I stayed up under Blaze and Ghost for the next two months. I just couldn't leave their sides. Blaze was having a tough time getting her energy back. Every time she felt that she was getting her strength back, she'd nurse Ghost and fall right back into exhaustion. I asked her if she wanted to feed him formula, but she'd strongly decline. It was getting the better of me. I didn't know what to do so I tried to do everything I could possibly think of to assist her. I held her and rocked with her. I answered her every beck and call. I tended to her and my son. I even gave her massages, so she'd go to sleep afterward. At the same time, I didn't want her to feel like she was alone.

From that, it was one bit of drama after the next. That shit was getting on my nerves when I was with Princess. I was at a point in my life where I adjusted to being the best father to my kids and to give them the best life that I possibly could. I was starting to see things clearer, especially when looking into my children's eyes.

About a month after me and Blaze had gotten back from the hospital with our son, I was walking Ghost down the hallway upstairs when I came across Princess' bedroom door. It was slightly ajar. Something told me to nudge it in just a little bit, so I did. What I saw made me lose my mind.

Princess was sitting on the edge of the bed with Silas kneeling in front of her holding a mirror that had powder on it. She took a straw and put it inside her nostril, tooting the line real hard before doing the same with the other nostril. When she was done, she pulled on her nose, laughed and laid back on the bed with a big smile on her face.

Silas took the straw and cleared two lines before setting the mirror aside and climbed on the bed to her. He kissed all over her neck and ran his hand under her short skirt. I could see his hand move in and out of her box.

I was so heated that my vision was hazy. The palms of my hands were sweating. My trigger finger got to itching and my heart was beating harder than ever. I was seconds away from rushing into the room and fuckin' both of them up, especially after seeing Jahliya sitting on the floor ten feet away from the bed, playing on her tablet as if nothing was going on behind her. I took two steps toward the door when my mother opened her bedroom door and called my name, snapping me out of my zone.

"Taurus! Come here for a second!" She waved me over to her.

I flared my nostrils and bit my bottom lip, watching Silas finger-fucking Princess so fast and so hard that she was writhing on the bed like a maniac. I nodded. "A'ight." I turned to my mother and walked into her room.

She closed the door after looking both ways in the hall.

I paced back and forth, ready to body a nigga.

She scrunched her face. "Baby, what's the matter with you?" She blocked my path and tried to place a hand on my chest.

I blocked it and slammed my fist into my hand. "Mama, I'm sick of this girl for real. I mean, I love her and all, but I'm over this drama. I need to get away from her before I wind up doing something I'm gonna regret." I started to imagine slumping Princess and that fool Silas. The killing her part didn't sit well with my heart, but it was how I was feeling. I didn't know what else to do.

My mother grew a worried look on her face. "Baby, that's one of the reasons I called you in here. I think it's time we all go our separate ways. You and Blaze need to be alone so y'all can raise your son together. I need to get back so I can help Danyelle with our business. Princess needs to take Jahliya and figure out what she's going to do with her own life. We cannot all stay under the same roof and expect it to work. That boy that Princess is dealing with got her doing drugs now. She's careless now and way too disrespectful around my grandbaby. Something has got to give. On top of that, I don't trust her around Blaze. I think she gon' end up doin' something to that girl."

I shook my head. "Like I said, I love Princess, but if anything happens to Blaze, ma, I swear to God you gon' see a side of me that you've never seen before. She's who I really want to be with. She reminds me so much of you."

My mother smiled. "Then, if that's who you choose, why don't you have a sit down and get each of y'all on the same page. Tell Blaze in front of Princess, then let her know that you have to move on and y'all go y'all separate ways." She walked up to me and hugged me briefly. "It's time to become a real man, son."

***

That night, after my mother cooked a feast and filled all our stomachs to the max, we loaded into the big den downstairs to get an understanding. My mother, myself and Blaze were already present after eating out meals. Princess and Silas decided that they needed to take a whole hour before they came downstairs to join us. By the time they did, I was furious and ready to bust Silas in his shit since I vowed never to put my hands on Princess again.

They walked into the den, laughing all goofy. Silas had his arm around Princess' shoulders, kissing her on the cheek every few steps. When they walked past me, I was sitting on the couch next to Blaze. I could smell the scent of sex on them. That made me a lil' heated and jealous. I ain't gonna lie, I still couldn't stomach the fact that another nigga was fucking my baby mother. The memories of us being together flashed through my mind every time I saw them together. I still had feelings for her real tough. I think I always would. It was just one of those things.

They plopped down on the couch across from me and Blaze. Princess' short skirt rose above her thighs. Silas placed his hand on top of them, rubbing all over them while whispering in her ear.

The kids were being tended to by the nannies so we could sit like adults and have this talk. I was irritated by their lateness and utter lack of respect that I stood up and kicked it off right away. "Look, the reason I called everybody here is because we all have to go our separate ways. My mother's going hers. Me and Blaze about to ours, and you two? I give a damn where you go but you gotta get up out of here. I'm serious. Doing dope and shit around my shawty? This nigga always touchin' you inappropriately like that and not caring who he doin' it in front of. Ain't either of you got respect for the rest of the people in this mansion. On top of that, it ain't my job to support grown ass niggas. I don't care what you talkin' 'bout, Princess. You know better."

She hissed through her teeth. "It sound like you just jealous, Taurus." She kissed his cheek and rubbed his chest.

"Look, Princess, he's right. We're adults here. We can't expect to live off Taurus forever. We have to find our own way. He's been generous enough, don't you think?" my mother asked, crossing her arms.

Princess frowned. "That nigga owe me his life, just like I probably owe him mind. I gave this man all of me and a whole daughter. What he do? He go and wife this bitch. She was supposed to stay his side chick, but I guess I was the side bitch all along." She looked over to Blaze and narrowed her lids.

"That's what I'm sayin', Princess. Look at how your mouth is in front of my mama. You have no respect for nobody. All you wanna do is play the victim. That shit getting real old."

"Princess, it ain't like that. Me and Taurus—" Blaze started.

"Shut up, bitch!" Princess waved her off and stood up after brushing Silas' arm from around her. "What you sayin', Taurus? You thinkin' you about to ride off into the sunset with this bitch while you leave me and my daughter behind to struggle? If so, that ain't gon' happen. I can't be happy, you can't either. We gon' reap the same benefit as Blaze and that pale ass baby y'all got. Fuck what you talking about." She balled her hands into fists.

I can't even lie; I felt like smacking the shit out of her, but I did my best to control my temper. I pushed her ass back to the couch. She fell on top of Silas. I was hoping that nigga would say something out of order. I was gon' make him pay for her sins. She bounced off the couch and tried to get in my face, but he pulled her back to the couch.

"Chill, bae. Look, P, he's right. We can't expect to live off him forever. We're adults here. let's just get the fuck up out of here. It's too much bullshit going down anyway. I don't wanna have to sweat this nigga about you. Feel me, shorty?" Silas held her to the couch and she tried her best to get from under him.

"Let me go, Silas! I'm tired of this nigga putting his hands on me! He don't even chastise that bitch like he do me. Get off me!" She pushed him and slid from under him. I thought she would jump back over to my side, but she picked up a glass case and threw it. It crashed into Blaze's knee and shattered across the floor. "If I can't have you then this bitch can't either!" Princess screamed and ran at Blaze after picking up a shard of glass.

Blaze jumped up in time. Princess was aiming the piece for Blaze's face. Just as Blaze held up her hand, the glass slammed right into it. "Princess what the fuck is wrong with you!" Blaze hollered with blood skeeting out of her palm.

Whap! Princess slapped her across the face and punched her. I grabbed her by the waist and threw her onto the sofa.

Silas hopped up and tackled me into the liquor cabinet. My back crashed through the glass. About ten bottles fell on top of my head. Before I could get myself together, Silas rained blow after blow into my face. "Bitch. Ass. Nigga. Don't. Put. Yo—"

Bam! My mother slammed a lamp into the back of his head, bussing it wide open. "Get off my son!"

He fell to his knees, dizzy. Blood ran down the back of his neck. It was all the distraction I needed. I shot up from the liquor cabinet with blood dripping from the scar on my forehead. I rushed him and kicked him square in the mouth. He leaned backward before he fell on his side and struggled to get up. But I was on his ass. I stomped him in the side of the jaw and punched him in the mouth, knocking him all the way to the floor where I was on him like a big ass roach that wouldn't die. I mean I brought my knee all the way up to my chest and brought my foot down on his skull.

"Baby, no!" my mother screamed, trying to pull me away from him.

I was fed up with him and Princess. Since I couldn't take my frustrations out on her, I made him the sacrifice. I kicked and stomped on him until he was lying in a puddle of blood. My socks were drenched with it. I saw that he wasn't moving. He was only laying on his chest, accepting my assaults. I took a step back and looked down on him. His neck was turned awkwardly. He had one eye open and the other was closed tight. Blood leaked out of his nose, mouth and the wounds that I'd caused in his head. I wanted to stomp his ass some more.

Blaze sat in the corner of the den with her knees to her chest. She had her face buried in her thighs. I could hear her whimpering.

Princess stood with blood coming from her lip. She slowly walked over to Silas and kneeled. She placed two fingers at his jugular and held them there, looking up at me. After not finding a pulse, she lowered her head and smiled. "You killed him, Taurus. Jealous ass nigga, you killed him." She stood up and looked up at me with watery eyes.

"That's his fault. That nigga ain't have no business getting into our business. It is what it is, Princess. You kicked this off."

She sucked on her bottom lip and nodded. "A'ight. That's how you wanna play it, right? Okay. Then let's do it." She ran out of the den so fast that I couldn't grab her.

My mother's eyes got big. She rushed over to Blaze. "Come on, baby, get up. That girl is crazy. I got to get you out of here."

I rushed out of the den in pursuit of Princess. I caught her taking the stairs two at a time. I was right behind her. She got all the way to the room and tried to close the door but before she could, I pushed it open, knocking her backward. She crawled halfway to the bed and pulled a Steve Madden shoebox from underneath it, recovering a .9-millimeter handgun. She cocked it and aimed it at me.

I closed the door behind me and stepped further into room, clenching my jaw. "What you waitin' on,

Princess? Gon' 'head and pull the trigger," I encouraged her.

She steadied herself on her feet and wrapped both hands around the gun. Tears flowed from her eyes. "Taurus, get out of my way. I'm finna kill that bitch, and you ain't gon' stop me."

I shook my head. "I can't let you do that, Princess. You and I both know that this has very little to do with Blaze. We were never right for each other. We chose to cross those lines because we were in our *fuck the world* mode. But when it all boiled down, we don't have nothin' in common but the streets. I need more than that, Princes. So do our children." I took a step forward, baiting her.

I didn't know what I was thinking. I knew that she was just as crazy as I was. I'd watched her buss her gun with no remorse. A part of me wanted her so I could feel some sense of relief from putting my hands on her, or maybe even for breaking her heart. I still loved that woman and I would never forgive myself for some of the things I'd done to her.

She blinked, and tears slid down her brown cheeks. She shook her head and inhaled. "Taurus, you choosin' that bitch over me after all we've been through. I'm supposed to be your right hand. I been with you through it all. Now this is how you're going to repay me. I can't let you do us like this. Me and my daughter deserve so much better." She raised the gun, aiming at my face.

My eyes became misty. I felt like my heart was ripping in two. Images of our past flashed through my mind. The beef with Juice. My father, Gotto. Her father, Donnell. Nastia. Princess had been with me through it all, riding beside me, ready to die. I'd never met another human being on earth that had as much heart as she did.

"Princess, I swear on my mother that I love you. I love you with all my heart and soul, but I know that we are not good together. It's always going to be this back and forth, tit for tat type shit, and I need more than that. I gotta be a father to these children now. This street shit gotta cease to exist. If I stay with you, we gon' be on the same ol' thing. We have to advance. Our children's future depends on it. Can't you see that?" I took another step toward her.

She took a step back and kept the gun leveled. "You won't give me no credit, Taurus. You just think I'm some hood chick that'll never make it out of the slums. Don't you know that I want better for myself and my daughter, too? You're the one that pursued me! You said that you didn't want me leaving your side. That you'd be my daddy for life. That you would never leave my side. You lied to me! I hate you so much right now!" She cried harder.

I felt the tears sliding down my cheeks. I closed my eyes and lowered my head to my chest. I didn't know what to do. I was caught up, dazed and confused. I pushed the gun out of my face and pulled her to me, holding her in my arms while she cried against me. I didn't know what to do, think or how to make it better. I still loved Princess too much to let her go. At the same time, I loved Blaze just as hard. I had Silas' dead body downstairs, two women that hated each other, and two children by each one of those women. I was lost.

"Princess, I don't know what to do. I know you're used to me having all the answers, but I don't have them this time. All I know is that I don't want to lose you and my daughter. I want the both of you. We will figure this out. I just don't know." I kissed the side of her forehead and held her in my arms.

"I can't do this, Taurus, it's way too much for me. It's killing me slowly. I swear I can't do this shit anymore." She cried. "I think it's best we all parted for real. It's the only way." She pushed me off her and dropped to her knees. Then, she placed the gun on the floor and covered her face with her hands. She was sobbing loudly. "I gotta get out of here, Taurus. I need to get as far away from you as possible until I can get my mind right. I need you to keep Jahliya. She's a constant reminder of you and I just can't take that right now."

Chapter 12

It was three in the morning that same night. Me and Hood Rich were on our knees in the basement, hacking away at Silas' limbs. The light bulbs in the basement had been red ones. Just like my mother's crib back in the day. We'd already slit both of his wrists and his stomach down the middle, along with his neck so his blood could drain out of him, down the hole in the tub. I'd kept him that way for five hours. That's when Hood Rich showed up and I told him what happened. He pressed the trigger of the chainsaw and brought it to Silas' shoulder before cutting the right a one clean away from his body. After he removed that one, he went to the other shoulder and did the same thing while I pulled on Silas' wrist until his arm had come completely off.

Hood Rich turned the chainsaw off and pulled his protective glasses over his head. "Taurus, I told you a long time ago that you had to honor the women, man. It's the only way. You tellin' me you're about to let Princess leave?" His eyes got bucked. "Nigga, y'all have been through way too much together. It ain't my business but I think that's a bad idea. You only find female versions of cats once in a life time. It ain't that many. Hold that nigga leg out for me." He pulled out the chainsaw and got back to work.

After we finished dicing Silas into a bunch of pieces, we hopped in Hood Rich's Range Rover and headed to the swamps on Forest Creek Road. He took a long, dark path into the woods when it began to rain. I was laid back in my seat, deep in thought.

Every time I saw Princess' face in my mind, I got sick and to puke my guts.

Hood Rich laid a hand on my shoulder. "Taurus, y'all gon' figure this shit out. On the flipside, it's time we move in on Kilroy. I got everything in place for us to take this nigga down. Since you been doing your thing, I been slowly crippling him, two traps at a time. You already know that once you hit a nigga pockets the right way, you strip him of power. That's what I did. Now, I need you by my side when I smash this nigga." He pulled off the road and onto a mud path that led to an embankment, then stopped the truck where we got out.

It was kind of cool that night. The rain drizzled from the pitch-black sky. It smelled like a dirty fish tank. I could taste the salt of the water in the air. I gripped two black bags and followed Hood Rich. He led me to a bridge. Once there, one by one we tossed the pieces of Silas over the rails, watching the gators basically fight over him as they splashed about in the murky water.

"I got a few niggas I want you to meet, Taurus, that's gon' help you get rich out here in Miami. Killas, too. After you get your house squared away we need to get back to the money." He dumped his entire bag over the side of the bridge.

I did the same thing. Silas' body parts splashed into the water. I could hear the gators groaning and chomping loudly.

"A house divided can't stand, Hood Rich. Before I do anything else, I must see to it that my women are squared away. I made enough stupid ass decisions already."

We made our way back to the truck and burned the plastic bags before wiping out arms down with a cloth that was drenched in rubbing alcohol. Then, we got back into the truck, when his phone blared.

He looked at the face and began typing real fast on the digital keyboard. "I need you to roll out to the docks with me. There is a shipment there that I need to pick up. It's urgent. He finished typing and sat the phone between his legs, looking over at me.

I nodded and pulled my seatbelt across my chest. I closed my eye, lost in through while Hood Rich pulled off. Before I left the house that day, Princess had started to pack her things. Watching her do it hurt me so bad that I felt like breaking down and snatching her lil' ass up to tell her to stay. I envisioned me being out in this cold world without her. Ever since she came into my life I'd been her protector. I refused to allow anything to happen to her. I'd put my life on the line to ensure that hers never came into jeopardy. We'd accrued a bunch of deadly enemies along the way. Now, she was set to be out there all alone. If anything happened to her, I would never forgive myself. I exhaled through my nostrils.

***

Twenty minutes later we arrived at the docks, right off Pike Bay behind South Beach. Hood Rich pulled up and took his .45 from under his seat. He put it under his shirt. "Taurus, make sure you're strapped. These Haitian niggas are crazy, and I don't trust them." He opened his door and stepped out.

I already had a .40 Glock on me. I got out of the truck and stood about, watching Hood Rich walk up on a dark-skinned dude with long dreads that had red tips on the ends of them. They shook hands. Behind him was another dark-skinned man who had a Mach .11 in his hand. He watched me and Hood Rich closely while he stood on the side of their Benz Truck with the concern. I started to imagine having a shootout, and him being able to hide behind the passenger's door while he busted at us. He was in the perfect position to cause the most damage. I couldn't allow for that to happen.

"Say, Hood Rich. Tell homeboy to close that door. It don't look right to me." I took the .40 out of my lower back and held it at my side, since he had his gun out. He wasn't about to have the ups on me. I didn't give a fuck what this meeting was about. I had kids to live for now.

Hood Rich looked over the Haitian's shoulder and frowned. "Yeah, Pony, why don't you tell ya' mans to close that door and put the Mach up. This is a friendly atmosphere."

Pony shook his head. "I am a prince. This is how I'm protected. He's only doing his job. Act as if he's not here. It's easier that way." He looked back at his security.

I raised my pistol and shut my right eye, aiming that bitch right at the man's forehead. Any false move and I was blowing his wig off. "A'ight then. Until this meeting is over, this how we gon' roll. Handle yo' business, big home."

Hood Rich nodded and shielded his eyes from the moon as he scanned the area.

There was a big ass boat docked that was gray with seaweeds matted to the side of it. It looked like a medium-sized yacht. One that had not been kept up in the best conditions. The rain tapered off. There were what seemed like a million little bugs flying around in our faces. The water smashed into the boat. In the distance was a loud horn and a lighthouse. I had a very eerie feeling about that place.

"There are ten women, fifteen kids, and ten men inside of this boat that you are responsible for. I am to understand you have already received the proper payment for this task?" Pony asked, before swatting at a bunch of little bugs that were crawling all over his face.

I had a few crawling on my neck that I smashed with my open palm. I was itching like crazy, but kept my aim pinned on the security dude.

Hood Rich nodded. "Everythang is good on my end. Hope you made sure that the men are ready to go to war beside me like I was promised they would be back in Kingston. Long as they follow my directives accordingly, their families will be well taken care of. You can send me a boatload every other week. I can handle it." He looked over his shoulder at me. "Taurus, this is Pony. He's one of the major players I wanted you to meet. We gon' need him before you get established down here in Miami. He runs the top portion."

I kept my aim and nodded in a what's up fashion at Pony. "Say, Hood Rich. You said this dude is Haitian, but to my understanding, that's a boat full of Jamaicans, right?" I asked.

Hood Rich nodded again. "Yeah, we're right off the islands that surround the States. Pony got a say in that, which is why I need for you and him to get acquainted. It's good. You can put that gun down."

As soon as he said that, I saw the lights of a semitruck driving down the same dirt path that we had taken. Dust flew up from its tires as it got closer.

"What the fuck is that?" I nodded in the direction of the truck with my gun still on Pony's shooter.

Hood Rich looked over his shoulder at the approaching truck and pulled his .45 off his waist, cocking it. "All that's the transportation for this package that Pony just dropped off. If you stay ready, you ain't ever gotta get ready. Ain't that right, Prince of the Islands?"

Pony laughed and nodded.

The truck pulled up beside the boat. Four of Hood Rich's men jumped out of it with DSKs in their hands. One of them had his back to us. The next thing I knew, eight men dressed in all-black with long dreads appeared on the side of the boat with assault rifles in their hands. There was a light that came on in the middle of the deck on the yacht and in the back of the truck. Then, they were barking orders at them.

Pony walked over to me, extending his hand. I reluctantly shook and felt sick to my stomach. His hands were hot, sweaty and gross. "Taurus, you and I have to have a chance to sit down real soon. I'll fly you out to Port Au Prince in a month. It's the earliest my schedule opens. After we get a feel for another,

I'll be dropping heavy shipments in your lap. It's been cosigned by Hood Rich."

I shook his hand and released it. "That sound good. I can't wait until we can make that happen. I'll be looking forward to it."

Hood Rich came over and slammed his hand down on my shoulder. "Taurus, I need you to roll my truck back to my crib while I handle this business. I'll meet you there in about three hours. Hit my phone when you get there, and I'll pop he locks by use of my phone. A'ight?" He jogged away from me and jumped into the semi.

It stormed away, and I got behind the wheel of his whip and headed to his palace.

***

Four hours later, I met back up with Hood Rich. He'd taken me back to my pad. The sun was beginning to break through the night. It was five in the morning and I was beat.

"This Friday, that nigga Kilroy gon' be throwing a birthday bash for his twin daughters. They're turning sixteen. I want this party to be the last one he attends, if you get my drift." He grunted and looked up at the mansion. "I had to body that nigga Beast, too. He found about what happened to Quik and had speculations. Instead of waiting for him to make his move, I just bussed his brains. I want Philly for myself anyway. I'm thinking of flooding it with Jamaicans that'll run under me. Don't nobody push that heroin like Jamaicans, Taurus." He looked over at me.

I was hearing everything he was saying, but my eyes were on the mansion. I was dreading going inside. I didn't to all. All of Princess' shit wasn't going to be there. I tried not to let it fuck with my emotions. I wasn't ready for her to be out of my life.

"I'm gon' need you by my side. Even though I got a lot of niggas pledging their loyalty to me, I don't trust none of them to watch my back the way that I know you will."

"Well, you know I gotcha, bruh. I'll be there. You can count on that." We shook up and I got out of the whip and slammed the door, taking a deep breath before I made my way inside of the mansion.

When I got inside, Princess was standing at the marble counters, eating Cookie Crisp cereal. She had SZA's *Broken Clocks* playing out of the speakers. She had on a short blue laced nightgown that stopped just below her butt cheeks.

I walked around the counter and dropped my keys on top of it, right next to her. "Good morning. What you doin' here so early?" I asked, kissing her on the cheek.

She frowned and dropped the spoon in her bowl, then wiped her cheek. "Don't be puttin' your nasty ass lips on me. I don't know where they've been.," she snapped with her lips curled. She stood up and dropped the bowl into the sink. She rolled her eyes at me and walked out of the kitchen, mumbling under her breath.

I caught up to her just as she walked into her room. She was getting ready to close the door when I stopped it with my right hand. "Hold on. Let me holler at you for a second."

She sucked her teeth and walked further into the room. "You better not wake up Jahliya. It took me forever to get her to sleep. She's been crying for all night. It's irritating." She sat beside her on the bed and rubbed our daughter's back.

I sat beside her and lowered my head before looking over at her. "Princess, I ain't ready for us to be a part. I still love you with all my heart and it's killing me to imagine what life is going to be like without you being my right hand. We been through so much together."

She stood up and shook her head. "Damn, Taurus. Don't do this shit right now. You said that we all have to go our separate ways. Ever since you said that, I've been wrapping my head around doing my own thing. I know it's going to be hard, but I'd rather fail repeatedly than to sit back and watch you and that broad raise a son together. You have killed my soul, Taurus. I never thought I'd see the day when you chose another woman over me. I mean, you did it publicly. There was just a hint of my innocence left, and you took it. You stripped it away from me just so you could be with Blaze." She hung her head and was quiet for a long time. Her frown slowly turned into a smile. "But, you know what? It's time I get out here and do me. I have to find my own way. I've been screwed over by so many men. My family has hurt me in unimaginable ways, and yours has too. I'm in my twenties and I don't have anything to show for myself. How can I ever expect Jahliya to look up to me as a role model if I don't have anything to model?"

I stood up and face her. "Princess, you got me. You ain't gotta do nothin'. You know I'll go out there and make it happen for you and everybody else.

That's my nature. If you never wanted to work ever again, you would never have to. We got stupid chips put up. What the fuck I look like letting you work? You're supposed to be your own boss. You don't work under nobody."

"You got a whole ass other woman in this mansion whose finger you just put a ring on. She's expecting to be your wife. What part of that don't you understand?"

"What does that have to do with me taking care of you for the rest of your life and making sure you never have to work anybody, huh? Explain that to me?"

She shook her head. "You are not my man anymore. You're hers. You chose her right in my fucking face, in front of your mother and everything. Damn. As long as I allow you to pave the way for me, and make sure that I never have to get off my ass, I'll be a prisoner by you." She sat back on the bed and rubbed our daughter's back.

Jahliya started to move around. I guessed she figured she was on the verge of waking up and wanted to prevent that.

I kneeled before her. I couldn't take it no more. I took her left hand and held it. "Baby, I love you. I am not about to lose you. You are my rib. You know that. I would be broken without you beside me. Just tell me what I have to do. I'll absolutely do anything for you. I swear."

"You put a ring on that girl's finger. Out of all the stuff that we have been through, you never kneeled before me and put a ring on my finger. You've called me your wifey and all that other slick ghetto shit, but you never thought to make me your wife. I've always just been your right hand, hood chick. You saw Blaze and she appealed to you. You have two different views of us. Clearly, she's more suitable to be your wife than I am, so I gotta that one on the chin and find my own way."

My heart felt like she was ripping it to shreds with manicured nails. I felt sick, like I was losing my best friend. In a sense, I was. Everything that was saying made sense. The fact was that whole time we'd been out grindin', bussin' our gun back when we had to survive. During our downtime, I have never thought to make her my wife that way. I saw her as my ghetto queen. My wifey, but not the actual wife God intended for me to have. I felt that most females settled for the man having them as the wifey. They never stopped to think that most times it's just us men's way of keeping them in place until we found our actual wife. Princess had picked up on it before I had and that shattered me.

I looked up at her and rubbed the side of her of her face. "I'm not about to lose you. I've never had it all figured out. You know that. I tell you that all the time. I messed up on so many levels. I'm man enough to admit that. But you have to believe me when I tell you that I am crazy about you. I love you with everything that I am as a man. Most importantly, I'd rather die than to be without you. I mean that with my soul."

She shook her head as her eyes misted over, sucking on her bottom lip. She looked into my eyes. "Taurus, it's only so much a woman can take on her shoulders. I like I'm on the verge of losing my mind.

I'm not strong enough to endure what you're taking me through. You have to release me. I'm begging you. For my own sake. Can you let me go?" She grabbed both sides of my face with her small hands.

I grabbed her wrists and held them. "No. I never can and never will. I'd rather kill you first." I meant what I'd said with every fiber of my being.

There were three knocks at the door, then Blaze pushed it in. "Taurus, when you're done in here, we need to talk." She stepped back into the hallway and closed the door behind her.

I sighed again and dropped my head to my chest.

Chapter 13

By the time I made it to the other side of the mansion, Blaze had five Louis Vuitton suitcases opened on the bed and was taking clothes out of the dresser drawers, stuffing them inside the cases. "I'm out of here, Taurus. I don't want to hear none of that sweet talking stuff that you just put on her because I've heard it all before. You forget that I was in the sex industry. I been around top-notch pimps, both male and females. I can't believe that I fell for your games thus far. Man, I feel so stupid." She continued to pack while our son slept in the crib about ten feet away from the bed.

"Blaze, you not about to go no damn where. You can put them clothes back, so we can sit down and talk like grown folk."

She shook her head. "We don't have anything to talk about, Taurus. You're clearly still in love with Princess. I stood in that hallway and heard the whole conversation. She begged you to let her leave. Told you that she needs it too, and you told her that you would rather kill her. What type of stuff is that?" She stopped and looked at for a second. Then, she shook her head and went right back to packing. "That's not cool, man. Not cool at all."

I walked over to her and grabbed her by the wrist. "Will you just chill for a minute and hear me out? Damn." I shook her wrist a little because I was frustrated.

"Talk. Say what you have to say, but I'm telling you now that there is nothing you can say to convince me to stay in this nightmare. I deserve better and so does Ghost. We can't raise a child in this toxic atmosphere. It's so unhealthy. He has to have better than we've had."

"Baby, I'm telling you the same thing that I told Princess. I don't have all the answers. I never claimed to have had them. I care about both of y'all so much. It's not just about me, you or Princess. It's about these children, too. I'm considering the whole picture. I can't let you walk out of those doors either, Blaze. I need you. I need for all three of us to make this work. It shouldn't have to be that hard."

Blaze yanked her wrist away from me and continued to pack. "I get it now. You're just completely out of your mind. You're nuts. I don't know how I didn't see that before, but I do now and its mind boggling." She laughed to herself. "I'm out of here. If you haven't noticed already, your ring is sitting on the dresser. I don't care what you with it, but it doesn't belong on my finger."

"What do I have to say to get you to understand that I am very confused right now? I'm not trying to lose either one of you. I get that I can't have both. That makes sense but it's still hard for me to let go. I'm struggling."

Princess opened the door and stepped into the room. "You're not struggling, Taurus, you're just selfish. You want us both and you don't want us to have nobody but you. That's very, very selfish. I feel like we've been puppets in your little sideshow for way too long. There are kids involved now. We have to set a better example for them. Especially Jahliya because she's old enough to understand something is wrong. She's been having nightmares ever since you killed Silas." She brushed past me and stood on the side of Blaze. "Hey, I just want to apologize to you. None of this is your fault. We have to stop letting Taurus play on our emotions because if we continue to let him, somebody is going to get seriously hurt. We can't have that. So, I'm apologizing to you as a woman and I'm open to Jahliya having a strong bond with Baby Ghost. I can't tell that she loves him already. He's her brother, and none of this is their fault."

Blaze dropped a stack of clothes in one of the suitcases and shook Princess' hand. "I appreciate you saying that, Princess, because you really didn't have to. I apologize for the pain that I have caused you as well. I knew, and Taurus were together when he and I started. I should have been more woman about it and stayed away, but I didn't. Now we're here." She looked over at me and shook her head. "I will also do my part to make sure that Ghost and Jahliya have the strongest relationship they possibly can have." She pulled Princess' hand inward to give her a hug.

Princess pulled away and placed her hand on her chest. "We're good, but you still basically killed me a few months back. I haven't gotten over that just yet. We'll take baby steps." Princess stepped away from her and look to me. "Now what are you going to do, Taurus? You got two women who are on the same page. That's got to be the worst thing for a player, right now." She laughed to herself and made her way out of the room.

My mother appeared in the doorway. "Before either of you decide, I want the three of us to have a girl's night out. Let's let our hair down and figure some things out. How does that sound?" She asked them.

Princess shrugged. "Sound good to you, Blaze?"

"Mama, I love you, and I love your son. I'm willing to sit down and listen to any advice that you have to give me, just as long as you are impartial. I think we both need a bit of your wisdom right now more than ever."

My mother stepped further into the room and hugged both women one at a time. I was so sick that I didn't know what to say or do. All I knew was that I wasn't about to lose neither one of my women. I refused to take that L. Like I told Princess, I'd rather die first.

* * *

It was real tense for the next couple of days. Me and Blaze said very few words to one another. Whenever we'd be in the same room, she'd go and stay on her side of the room and act as if she were engrossed in her cellphone, or tablet. I felt emotionally sick. Every time I thought about saying something to her I wound up second guessing it and saying nothing at all. Apart of me wanted to reach out and grab her to my body. Just hold her. I missed having her in my arms. Even though me and Princess were on the outs, she was as cool as a fan. She laughed with me, joked, and kept thing light and casual. But whenever I tried to cross that line by hugging her or putting my lips anywhere on her body, she broke that shit up right away and told me to not get things twisted.

It wasn't long before I was seriously miserable in that mansion. I was hoping that after my mother sat them down, she'd talk some sense into them. I couldn't stand to being without either one, and I was hoping my mother had a remedy.

Hood Rich came over to scoop me up late one Thursday, so we could handle the business back in Philly. I was ready to go and kill up as many niggas as I possibly could because I was emotionally, and internally hurting so bad.

As I heard him blowing his horn out in my driveway downstairs, I kissed Blaze on the cheek and was on my way out of the room when she hopped out of the bed and blocked my way. "Wait. before you leave, Taurus, take this with you." She handed me a gold locket that had a picture of myself, her and our son inside of it. "I know that the last few days have been a little rough for everybody around here, but life is too short. I don't know what you're about to go out east and do, I can feel it in my heart that it's dangerous. Taurus, I swear I love you with all of me. As much as I hate to admit it, I'm not going anywhere. You're going to be my husband. I would have never given you a child if I didn't expect to be your wife. So, when you come back, I'll be here waiting for you." She wiggled her fingers in my face to show me that she'd slid the engagement ring back on her finger. "We're for life, Taurus. Our son deserves that." She hugged me tight and stood on the tips of her toes and kissed my lips.

I held her for a long time. "Thank you, baby. I love you, and when I get back we gon' make it official. I promise."

I kissed her lips again, then kissed our son, and headed down the hall. Jahliya saw me and ran and jumped into my arms. I kissed all over her pretty face and hugged her to my chest. "Daddy gotta go, but I'll be back in a few days mama, okay."

"Okay," she returned, hugging my neck tightly. "When you get back, we gon' go to Disney Land?"

I put her down, and Princess came out of the room and picked her up. "Yeah, baby. If that's where you wanna go, we'll go." I kissed her cheek, then held out an arm for Princess to walk under. She surprised me when she did.

Princess poked me in the chest. "Taurus, you make sure you keep that vest on, and project yourself. I trust Hood Rich, but he's an old nigga. Them cats out east play for keep so I know y'all on business. You wouldn't be leaving otherwise. Just be careful. I love you, too. Never think otherwise. I'd still die for you, nigga. Word is bond."

I hugged her tight and kissed her forehead. "I love you, baby girl, and I needed to hear you say that whether you believe it or not."

My mother came out into the hallway, tying her silk robe. She waited until me and Princess were done talking before she signaled for me to come over to her with her forefinger.

I sent Hood Rich a text that I would be down in ten minutes, then stepped into her room.

"All I wanna know, Taurus, is who are you planning on spending the rest of your life with? Once I know that, I will now how to guide these lil' girls in the right direction. So, make sure you choose wisely. Your decision is going to affect many lives."

I exhaled with my jaws puffed out. "To be honest, I don't know. Both of these women have my heart, and now I have children to think about. You know me more than anybody else on this earth. Deep in your heart, you know which one of them I'm supposed to be with. That's who I want. You choose for me. The one that will love me more than anybody else, that will uplift me, and help me to become the best man that I could possibly can become. My Eve. That is the one I should be with. I don't know which one that is, but you do."

She slowly nodded and smiled. "Okay, baby. Mama got this. Just promise me that whichever one you choose, you honor her, love and cherish her faithfully for the rest of your life, until death parts the two of you. Can you promise me this?"

I stood there thinking everything over that I needed to do. I had more faith in my mother than anybody walking this earth. I knew that she would make the right decision for me. Whichever one she chooses, she would be faithful, and I would loyal to her for the rest of my life. I was sure of that.

I looked into her eyes and smiled. "I promise, Mama."

Chapter 14

I slid the white ski mask down my face and adjusted gloves on my hands while I sat in the passenger's seat of the Dodge Durango that Hood Rich had parked in the back alley of Kilroy's twin daughter's sweet sixteen birthday bash. It was nine o'clock at night, hot, with a little breeze that gave us enough relief. There was a van parked behind us with Hood Rich's goons inside. They been given the order that we were going to go into the party and kill everything moving.

Kilroy was the main target, but we had to send a message to all of Philly of how he got down. We were supposed to be bodying the females, and we had argued about it for half hour to get it straight until I got a migraine and gave in. I didn't give a fuck what they did. I wasn't smoking no females or kids unless I saw one with a gun in her hands.

I slammed the thirty-round extended clips in into my .40 Glocks and sat them on my lap. The silencers were crewed into the barrels. I was ready to handle my business. I needed to blow off some steam. I was internally going through it and my mind was also reeling. I wanted to get back to the crib to find out who my mother had chosen for me. The anticipation was almost too much to bare.

Hood Rich, took out a vial of cocaine and dumped a portion on to the back of his hand, snorting the powder almost immediately. "You been real quiet, Taurus. You good, lil' homie?" He looked over at me then picked up his binoculars and looked toward the house.

"I'm good, bruh. Ready to get this shit over with so you can sit on Philly's throne, and I can get right in Miami. Pony told you he wanna have a sit down with me?"

Hood Rich sniffed and pulled on his nose. "Fuck that nigga, Taurus. All that shit I said in front of you, disregard every word. We don't need him. That nigga living on borrowed time, just like this fool, Kilroy." He frowned and placed the binoculars back in his lap. "Fuck is this? She supposed to give me the signal already." He picked up his phone and started to text with his thumbs real fast. "You know a nigga ain't got his house in order when his bitch is the one setting him up for failure. That's why I don't trust these hoes, lil' bruh. They ain't loyal. If you find one, you better cherish that shit, 'cuz it's rare." He looked over his shoulder at the van and nodded.

I looked out of the window. "What are we waiting on?" I was ready to get this shit over and done with. My finger was itching, and my heart had yet to stop beating fast. I only got like that when I knew something was up.

Hood Rich's phone buzzed. He looked down at it then picked up the binoculars and bit into his bottom lip. "Here we go. Since you was bussing my head about killing her shorties and shit I told ol' girl to make sure that she have as many out of that house as she could before nine fifteen. Two are in jeopardy, but at least it ain't a full house like it could have been." He handed me the binoculars.

I looked toward the back of the house and saw the backdoor open, then there were a bunch of girls leaving with horns in their mouths that they blew and party hats on their heads. Some of them had different skin colors; what I assumed were their mothers. They had gone inside. We waited for ten minutes so as many of them could clear out as possible before we hopped out of the Durango and ran down the alley toward the back of the house with Hood Rich's goons leading the way. We knew that Kilroy was about that life, so it would be common sense for him to have security on high alert, and even though Hood Rich assured me that he'd be slipping, I wasn't so sure.

Hood Rich's men hopped over the backyard's fence, one by one. I did the same. Three of the four men ran alongside the house so they could enter the front door. Hood Rich went with them. Me and the remaining ran to the backdoor with me leading the charge. I stood with my back against the wall of the house. I waved my hand for one of Hood Rich's musclebound Goons to kick the door in.

He nodded, took a step back, and right before he could slam his foot into the door, I heard what sounded like Hood Rich and them kicking in the front door. Then, gunfire erupted. The Good with me kicked in the door with two hard tries. It splintered and fell inward. Two of Hood Rich's Goons ran in ahead of me, and I followed behind the big goon that had kicked the door in. More gunfire ensued. I waited for ten seconds, before I ran in behind them. I took the stairs two at a time with my guns extended. When I got into the house, there was a man's body laying with two big holes in him on the floor. He had a party hat on his head, and tears on his face. I stepped over him and ducked.

Inside the house was filled with gun smoke. I could hear females screaming before more fully automatic weapons were popped. One of Hood Rich's goons fell backward, and I landed on his side. Holes decorated his neck as blood gushed out of the gunshot wounds. He shook on the floor in front of me so I hid on the side of the stove.

Another scream emanated from the front of the house. It was followed by more gun fire. The house lit up again and again with flashes from the fire of the barrels.

"A'ight, lay it down, fuck nigga! Lay down or I'll put on in your daughter!" Hood Rich hollered.

I left the stove and made my way to the hallway that led to the living room where they were. Down that long hall were two more of Hood Rich's men. They were laid on their stomachs, lifeless. A big puddle of blood formed under them. There were also three other bodies in the hallway. They had to be Kilroy's men. I made my way slowly down the hall, stepping over them. I could see, Hood Rich with his arm around a slender caramel-skinned little girl. She had a golden crown on her head with pink diamonds in it. Tears ran down her cheeks.

"What type of nigga shoot up a girl's sweet sixteen birthday party! That ain't street, nigga! That's bitch shit!" Kilroy hollered with two .9 millimeters in his hands.

I continued to slide with my back against the wall, making my way in their direction as slowly as I could. My heart was in my throat. The hairs on my arms stood up on end. I could smell a mixture of gunpowder and blood in the air.

Hood Rich jacked the little girl up even more and pressed his gun to her temple. "Drop that gun, Kilroy. You already know what it is. You gon' take this bullet for your shawty or I'ma smoke her ass and you gon' smoke me. What you wanna do?" Hood Rich taunted him.

None of this shit made sense to me. I felt like Hood botched this hit. Had it been up to me, it would have gone a lot smoother. I was regretting being there.

Kilroy extended his arm and pointed it at Hood Rich's head. "It is what it is, my nigga. Welcome to Philly."

The gun jumped twice in my hand as the bullets spat out of it and slammed into Kilroy's chest, knocking him backward. He fell over the table holding his chest.

Hood Rich flung Kilroy's daughter away from him, rushed to Kilroy and got to squeezing the triggers on his guns over and over again. They jumped in his hands. The shells popped into the air and landed on the carpet. Kilroy's daughter saw me in the hallways and screamed at the top of her lungs. I grabbed her and wrapped my hand around her mouth, carrying her into the room where there were about five females huddled together.

I tossed her inside and toward the females. "Everybody quiet and nobody gets hurt," I assure them, then closed the door.

I rushed back in the room where Hood Rich was talking on Kilroy's phones, then stuffed them into his pockets.

He stood up and jogged toward the front where two more of his men were laid out, riddled with holes and leaking blood. I was curious as to what had happened to them but didn't find out until later that night.

***

I sat on the edge of the hotel bed with my head down. Both guns were on each side of me. I was drained, and tired of it all. I didn't understand Hood Rich's tactics, and really nothing about the operation. To be honest, I just wanted to be back in Miami with my family. I was tired of the life. The killing and being a part of it all. I just wanted to settle down and raise my shorties at this point. The game has a way of taking the life out of you even when you're still breathing. That's how I felt. I felt that I had been in the game long enough. I was over it.

Hood Rich stepped out of the bathroom with a silver platter. There was about ten grams of cocaine on top of it. He sat on the love seat with the platter on his lap, chopping through it with a razorblade. He created two lines, dropped the razor, and picked up a red straw, snorting both lines. He sat back, pulling on his nose. "Taurus, you need a lil' pick me upper. You need to try this shit right here. It'll get you right, lil' bruh. Trust me." He tried to hand the platter to me while he sniffed loudly and wiped at nose with his hand.

I shook my head and nudged the platter away from me. "I'm good, Boss. I grew up watching members of my family tootin' that shit. It wasn't long before they were smoking it. Now they mostly hypes. I can't go out like that. I got a lot of responsibility now." I exhaled and looked through the pictures of my shorties on my phone. I was missing both Jahliya and baby Ghost like crazy.

Hood Rich shrugged. "Suit yourself, bruh. But you gon' need to do something because ever since we got here you ain't been yourself. I can tell that something is eating at you. What's on your mind?" He separated the dope into two piles and made four lines from each pile. He snorted a line up his right nostril with his eyes closed.

"Being honest with you, Hood Rich. I ain't fit to take Meech's spot, bruh. I think I done had enough of the game. I'm ready square up and do the family thing."

Hood Rich laughed and shook his head. "Stop playing, Taurus. I know you just fucking with me. Niggas like us can't leave the game alone. It's embedded too deep within our hearts. What you gon' do? Be a stay at home dad or some shit? Only fuck with one woman, even though it's a billion dimes out there?" He scoffed. "Bruh, you just going through something right now. Maybe you still tripping off of what took place with the females or something, but I'm letting you know right now that you can't survive without the game. Neither one of us can. I done brought them Jamaicans over and shit. I got my lil' niggas training them so they can work under you out there on the Port. It' ain't gon' take me long to lock down Philly now that Kilroy, and even Pancho, are out of the way. I'm talking a few months I need you to be beside me, nigga. You see how you saved my ass once again. Had you not been there, that nigga would have blown his daughter away and me." He shook his head and lowered it. "I would have gotten my ass whacked just like them other niggas. It seemed like Kilroy was waiting on us to show up. At least that's the feeling I got." Hood Rich sat the palette on the table and stood up, running his hands all over his face.

I sighed and shook my head. "I'm done with this shit, Hood Rich. I'm tired, bruh. I think it's in your best interest to find my replacement. My heart ain't in the game no more. It's with my family. You gotta respect that." I started to put my pistols on my hip. I was ready to get back to Miami. Whatever Hood Rich had in mind for the next day, he would have to figure that out on his own. I wasn't planning on being present.

He shook his head. "N'all, fuck that. You can't do me like that, Taurus. You're the only nigga out here I trust. We got too much shit to handle for you to give up on me now." He turned around to face me with anger written across his face. "I've been where you are before, Taurus, and I'm tellin' you that feeling passes. You just probably got a lot of spirits on you from the people you've killed. They're fucking with you, man, but it will pass. I can't afford for you to turn your back on me right now. In fact, I can't call it either. I have too much invested in you." His face turned into a scowl as he looked down on me.

I stood up and lowered my eyes with an angry frown. "So, what are you saying, bruh? You can't respect my decision?"

Hood Rich laughed to himself and ran his hand over his face again. He looked at me and laughed, then turned to me. "Taurus, you knew what you were getting into before we bussed the moves that we bussed. You think that just because you're ready to retire that all of the niggas and organizations that you screwed over gon' let you do that without coming for your head?" He sucked his teeth. "Yeah the fuck right. The only reason you been good this far is because of where I got you put up. If you ain't fucking with me no more, then that means that my protection is lifted as well. That's what you really want?"

I stepped into his face and looked into his eyes. I felt my heart pounding in my chest. I clenched my teeth over and over again. "What you saying, Hood Rich? Fuck beating around the bush."

Hood Rich curled his upper lip. "Nigga, I'm saying that you're either riding with me one hundred percent, or you're against me. There is no in between when it comes to the game. Never has been, and you know that." He looked into my eyes with his hands opening and closing into fists.

"Nigga, the deal was that if you helped me track down my mother and daughter, and brought that nigga Juice to me, that I would help you find Meech and body his ass. I did that. We not only knocked him off, but a list of other niggas in Chicago that I didn't know. shit about. So, if you ask me, we are more than even. I'm coming to you like a gangsta and telling you that this shit ain't in my heart no more. I'm done with it. As a man and my big homie, you should respect that shit, bruh, and encourage me to take care of my family. To go a different route and do something better with my life. But you're just like my father, Hood Rich. All you care about is you and what's in your best interests. That's weak, bruh, and you know it."

He balled his face. "You know you the only nigga I let talk to me the way that you do, Taurus. Any other nigga, I'da already knocked his head off of his shoulders Chiraq style."

I scoffed and nodded. "So, what, now? How we finna have this?" I wasn't trying to be having a long drawn out discussion with him over what I wanted to do with my life. It was clear that he wasn't seeing things my way. His true colors were coming to the light for me. It had always been all about him to begin with. I saw that now.

He stepped away from me and shook his head. "It ain't gotta be no bad blood between us, Taurus. You ain't never did shit to cross me, bruh. I'm sicker than anything because I had plans for how we were going to take over some shit, but if your heart ain't in it no more, then it just ain't. I gotta honor that." He sat down and picked up the platter. "You can keep that mansion, lil bruh. That fifty mill has already been wired to your Swiss account, and as far as I'm concerned, you're always gon' be my lil' brother. Shit finna be hard for you in the beginning because we have amassed so many enemies, but I got you and your people. Trust and believe that. I appreciate you for saving my life on more than one occasion. I can never repay you for that, but I'll do my best. I also wish you all the best." He stood up and put the platter down, extending his hand to me.

I shook it and pulled him in for a half hug. "I love you, big homie. No matter whatever happens in life, never doubt that. And I appreciate everything that you have done for me as well. I just gotta get my life together. It ain't about just me no more."

He broke our embrace and nodded. "Man, gone home and take care of them women, homie. You gotta go hard for them and your kids, man. Teach 'em better than what we were taught. It's the only way."

I agreed.

It was hard for me to sleep that night. I laid on my back with my eyes open, watching the ceiling fan spin around and around. I was trying to come up with a way where myself, Blaze and Princess could love under the same roof in peace and harmony. I wanted Jahliya and Ghost to have the strongest relationship possible. I wanted to make sure that both of my children were given the maximum amount of opportunities to succeed in this cold, cold world. Next to them was Blaze and Princess. I knew that I needed to invest in them. To help them to obtain their goals and dreams. I couldn't continue to weigh them down with my mind games and inconsistent love and respect. I owed them more than that, and as hard as it was going to be, I was ready to render it to them with everything that I had. I also had to find my own way.

Ever since I was a little kid, all I've ever wanted to be was a King Pin. A street nigga. A dope boy. Somebody that had lots of women and money. I felt like I'd accomplished that. Saw what it was to be at the top of the game, and I didn't like what I saw. The more money you made, the more people you had to hurt. I understood that in order for one to advance, hundreds had to fail, or even die. I'd taken enough lives, corrupted enough women, and ripped apart too many families. I wanted to be forgiven for my sins and allowed to move on to do better with my family. So that night, I got down on my knees and begged God for forgiveness through tears. I felt that the weight of the world was coming off my shoulders while I confessed my sins to the heavens. I began to shake uncontrollably. My heart was pounding, and my head was spinning. All of the wrongs that I'd done played before my mind's eye. With every revelation I felt weaker and weaker. It caused me to cry out even harder. I was glad that Hood Rich had decided to spend the night out with one of his Philly chicks because I needed to get all is out of me.

Once I finished breaking down, I jumped in the shower so I could cleanse my body as well as my soul. After I jumped out, it was easier for me to fall right to sleep because I was so depleted.

Chapter 15

I didn't get back into Miami until the next night, at eleven o'clock. I was more than ready to see my girls and find out which one of them my mother had chosen for me. On the flight over I'd spoken with my mother and she'd assured me that I was going to be more than happy with her decision. She'd said that not only had she picked the right woman for me, but that both Blaze and Princess had agreed on it collectively. The suspense was literally killing me. It was hard for me to be still in my seat as we flew over the states that led down to Florida.

Hood Rich gave me a half hug before I got out of his Navigator limousine. "Bruh, you know I'm just a phone call away. Anything you need, don't hesitate to get at me, and I got you."

I hugged him tighter and patted his back. "The same here, big homie. You know I'm done with the game, but if ever you need a rider by your side to watch your back when you can't trust nobody else, I'll be there for you. That's what loyalty is." I stepped out of the limo and we shook up before the Navigator pulled out of the drive way. Hood Rich raised the window and sparked a blunt. I could see the flame through the tints.

I watched the brake lights as his limo disappear down the street until they were out of sight. Then I turned around and walked up the long driveway to my mansion, feeling a sense of relief that the game was finally about to be behind me. I was headed to a new life. A new beginning where I would do so many things differently. I had to make things right with my girls. Had to let them know that from here on out I would cherish, honor, and respect them like my life depended on it because I felt like it did.

Taking a deep breath, I put the key into the lock of the door before pushing it open. Once in, I kicked the door closed behind me, and immediately an eerie feeling came over me. Darkness had consumed the mansion and the only sounds I could hear were Jahliya screaming at the top of her lungs, throwing a fit like something was wrong with her.

I frowned, dropped my keys on the marble countertop, and stepped further into the mansion, allowing my eyes to adjust to the darkness. "Princess, why is my daughter crying like that? Where are y'all at?" I hollered, starting to get irritated. I couldn't stand hearing Jahliya cry. It always hurt my soul. My daughter had been struggling with ear infections ever since she was born. I was thinking she may have been suffering from one of them this night.

"We're in the living room, baby!" My mother called out from the back of the mansion.

I made my way in the direction of her voice. As I walked past the kitchen, there were lots of candles on each side of the hallway that led into the living room. Because of them, I was able to see where I was going. Jahliya started to scream louder, then Ghost started. Now I had two of my children screaming at the top of their lungs. The noises were driving me up the wall. I was ready to snap.

I sped up the pace, got into the doorway of the living room, and nearly had a heart attack. My eyes got bucked, my heart fell to my stomach. I felt so weak that my legs buckled underneath me, causing me to stumble to the floor on my hands and knees.

The living room had candles all around it. It looked as if somebody was trying to perform a séance. But that's not what made me buckle. In the middle of the living room floor was my mother.

She sat crossed-legged, Indian style, wearing a short night gown that stopped at the top of her thighs. Blaze was laid out on the right side of her with blood pouring out of a long gash in her throat. Her head lay in a puddle of her own blood. She wore a similar night gown to my mother, but it was drenched in blood. On the left side of my mother was Princess. She was also laid out on her back. Her throat was slit in the same fashion as Blaze's. Her eyes were wide open and unseeing. She had a shocked look on her face. Her mouth hung open. In the front of my mother was the knife.

In the back of her, seated in the middle of a bunch of couch pillows, was Jahliya and Ghost. She had duct taped Jahliya's wrists and ankles together.

My mother smiled. Her eyes were bucked and glossy. She held up her left hand, and the flickers from the candles caused her hand to sparkle, showcasing the ring that I had proposed to Blaze with. "Come in, baby. See, mama has chosen herself for you, son. There is nobody that can love you the way that I can. You belong to me." She snapped.

I rushed over to Princess' side and cradled her in my arms. I laid my hand on her chest to see if there was any sign of a heartbeat. After finding none, tears began to pour from me. "Mama, what the fuck have you done?" I hollered, crawling over to Blaze after setting Princess back down and closing her eyes.

The floor was completely covered in blood. It felt like hot syrup. The scent was burnt plastic and spoiled milk. Blaze felt heavy in my arms. The gash in her neck was about seven inches long. It oozed her blood in thick dribbles, leaking onto me. I cried harder and rocked back and forth with her as my children screamed behind me.

"It has to be me, Taurus. I don't know what to do in that world without you. I can't allow for either one of those little girls to take my baby away from me. You were going to let me go. You never asked me to stay, not one time!" She hollered and stood up.

I sat on my bottom and pulled Princess over to me. I held her and Blaze in each arm and cried my heart out.

My mother picked up the knife and looked over to Jahliya and Ghost. The candles flickered all around. They made her shadows dance off of the walls of the living room. She blinked tears. "It's supposed to be us, Taurus! You and me and nobody else. I need you more than them. Nobody can love you the way that I can, and you know it!" She hopped over the couch and kneeled in front of my children, raising the knife above her head, ready to bring it crashing down into Jahliya.

I don't know how I made up the distance, but somehow, someway, my instincts kicked in. I dropped both women and bounced to my feet, hopped over the couch and tackled her before she could kill my daughter.

The knife flew out of her hands and slid across the floor. She punched and kicked at me. "Let me go, Taurus! I gotta kill them too! They can't be here! You ain't gonna love *no one* more than me! No! I can't take that! I just can't!" She screamed.

I grabbed her around the neck and squeezed with both hands. "What the fuck is wrong with you, mama! Why did you do this to them?" I cried. I felt like I was in some kind of a nightmare. The world seemed to be going in slow motion. I was having an out-of-body experience as I choked her.

She brought her knee up and slammed it into my nuts, sending them up into my stomach.

I hollered out in pain and fell off of her. "Mama! Aw, fuck!" I was out of breath and ready to throw up. I'd never been in so much pain in all of my life.

She jumped up and took off running full speed toward the front of the house. "You can't do this to me, Taurus!"

I crawled over and picked up the knife, using it to cut the duct tape off of my children before dropping it to the floor. I was still weak from her attack as Jahliya jumped on me and wrapped her arm around my neck, crying at the top of her lungs.

"Daddy, my mommy got an ow-ee. My mommy got an ow-wee; look, Daddy." She cried, pointing to Princess, who was surrounded in blood.

Ghost was also throwing a fit. His pale face had turned a bright shade of red. He squeezed his eyes tight while he wailed. I held him close to my chest, struggling to stand up. The blood caused the floor to become very slippery with minimal traction. I knew I had to get my babies to safety.

My mother had lost her mind. There was no telling what she was going to do next.

I'd just made my way to my feet when the front door busted open, and what seemed like a hundred police ran inside of the mansion with their guns out and pointed them directly at me. "Freeze! Get down on the ground right now, Taurus! Do it now! We don't want to do this to you," ordered one cop, holding a Mossberg pump in his hand.

My mother forced her way in between them, acting like a maniac. "He killed those girls. He killed them. I watched him cut their throats. Why would you do that, Taurus? How could you?" She fell to her knees, crying hysterically.

I slowly kneeled with both of my babies in my arms. "Look, man, I ain't trying to go there with y'all. Just make sure my kids aren't hurt, and don't put them in her care. She ain't right, right now." I slowly took my arms from around Jahliya and Ghost.

As soon as I did, the police rushed me and slammed me to the floor aggressively. Blaze and Princess's blood puddled around my face. They took the guns off my waist before snatching me up and whisking me off to their jail as my daughter cried out for me.

***

Six months later, I sat beside my attorney as my mother took the stand and gave a false account of what took place that night. She told the jury that she'd awaken that night to the sounds of me arguing with both women. I threatened over and over that if they didn't shut their mouths that I was going to kill them, and eventually did. She said she watched from the top of the stairs as I grabbed Blaze and slit her throat, before chasing Princess down and doing the same thing to her. Afterward, I laid them beside one another, apologizing to them for doing what I did.

According to her, I had been planning on killing my children next and fleeing the country in a private jet that somebody named Hood Rich had given me. I was on the run from Memphis where I'd killed more than a few people down there as well. She told them everything that she could think of.

I was found guilty on two counts of first degree homicide and was sentenced to death. Before my mother had gotten off the stand, she looked me in the eyes and smiled. "You reap what you sow, Taurus. This is nobody's fault other than your own."

Chapter 16

Ghost

They executed my father, Taurus, on June 20th of 2018. He was murdered by lethal injection and was taken away from me and my sister, Jahliya. Before my pops passed, I had the privilege of spending hours and hours of visiting with him and talking to him on the phone where I was able to chronicle his entire life. He'd been through so much and seen so many things that it's going to be impossible for me to run out of material to write about.

After my father was taken away to prison, Jahliya and myself were taken in by my aunt Danyelle. We were raised in Jackson, Mississippi. I'd be lying if I said that all the craziness had stopped there because it didn't. Danyelle was nothing more than a slightly less crazy version of my grandmother. So, you can already imagine some of the things that I went through growing up under her.

To this day, Jahliya and myself haven't had much contact or communication with my grandmother. She'd admitted time and time again the she was sorry for setting my father up. That she'd allowed for her emotions to get the better of her, and if she could go back and change things she would have never crossed those sexual lines with him to begin with.

My father had run into Ca$h somewhere along the way while he was on lock. It turned out that they'd known each other somewhat and had done some major business in the game. After my father was sentenced to be executed, I'd always told him that I was interested in writing a book about his life, and that of my own. He helped me to link up with Ca$h, and Ca$h put me in tune with his COO, Shawn, and the rest is history.

I was told that my old man was a pure goon that had a weakness for women. It would be that weakness that would ultimately cost him his life, and the lives of mine and my sister's mother. I know this story has been kind of crazy, and at times even mouth-droppingly unbelievable. But I gave it to y'all like my old man gave it to me. Uncut.

Thank you for taking the time out to dive into the life of my father, Taurus. Part of me wanted to place blame on this world, and the cards that were dealt to him. His life had been fucked up since birth, but a system cannot fail those it wasn't designed to protect. In my opinion, from the day he stepped foot on this Earth, he never had a chance.

THE END

Raised as a Goon 5

Submission Guidelines:

Submit the first three chapters of your completed manuscript to ldpsubmissions@gmail.com, **Subject line: Your book's title**. The manuscript must be in a .doc file and sent as an attachment. Document should be in Times New Roman, double spaced and in size 12 font. Also, provide your synopsis and full contact information. If sending multiple submissions, they must each be in a separate email.

Have a story but no way to send it electronically? You can still submit to LDP/Ca$h Presents. Send in the first three chapters, written or typed, of your completed manuscript to:

LDP: Submissions Dept
Po Box 870494
Mesquite, Tx 75187

DO NOT send original manuscript. Must be a duplicate.

Provide your synopsis and a cover letter containing your full contact information.

Thanks for considering LDP and Ca$h Presents.

Raised as a Goon 5

Coming Soon from Lock Down Publications/Ca$h Presents

BOW DOWN TO MY GANGSTA
By **Ca$h & Jamaica**

TORN BETWEEN TWO
By **Coffee**

BLOOD OF A BOSS **IV**
By **Askari**

BRIDE OF A HUSTLA **III**
THE FETTI GIRLS **III**
By **Destiny Skai**

WHEN A GOOD GIRL GOES BAD **II**
By **Adrienne**

LOVE & CHASIN' PAPER **II**
By **Qay Crockett**

THE HEART OF A GANGSTA **II**
By **Jerry Jackson**

LOYAL TO THE GAME **IV**
By **T.J. & Jelissa**

A DOPEBOY'S PRAYER **II**
By **Eddie "Wolf" Lee**

THE BOSS MAN'S DAUGHTERS **III**
By **Aryanna**

TRUE SAVAGE **III**
By **Chris Green**

IF LOVING YOU IS WRONG… **II**
By **Jelissa**

BLOODY COMMAS **II**
By **T.J. Edwards**

A DISTINGUISHED THUG STOLE MY
HEART **II**
By **Meesha**

ADDICTIED TO THE DRAMA
By **Jamila Mathis**

Available Now

RESTRAINING ORDER I & II
By **CA$H & Coffee**
LOVE KNOWS NO BOUNDARIES I II III
By **Coffee**
RAISED AS A GOON I, II & III
By **Ghost**
LAY IT DOWN I & II
LAST OF A DYING BREED
By **Jamaica**
LOYAL TO THE GAME
LOYAL TO THE GAME II
LOYAL TO THE GAME III
By **TJ & Jelissa**
BLOODY COMMAS
By **T.J. Edwards**
IF LOVING HIM IS WRONG…
By **Jelissa**
PUSH IT TO THE LIMIT
By **Bre' Hayes**
BLOOD OF A BOSS I II & III
By **Askari**
THE STREETS BLEED MURDER I, II & III
THE HEART OF A GANGSTA
By **Jerry Jackson**
CUM FOR ME
CUM FOR ME 2
CUM FOR ME 3
An LDP Erotica Collaboration
BRIDE OF A HUSTLA I & II
THE FETTI GIRLS I & II
By **Destiny Skai**

WHEN A GOOD GIRL GOES BAD
By **Adrienne**
A GANGSTER'S REVENGE I II III & IV
THE BOSS MAN'S DAUGHTERS
THE BOSS MAN'S DAUGHTERS II
A SAVAGE LOVE I & II
BAE BELONGS TO ME
A HUSTLER'S DECEIT I, II
By **Aryanna**
A KINGPIN'S AMBITON
A KINGPIN'S AMBITION II
I MURDER FOR THE DOUGH
By **Ambitious**
TRUE SAVAGE
TRUE SAVAGE II
By **Chris Green**
A DOPEBOY'S PRAYER
By **Eddie "Wolf" Lee**
WHAT ABOUT US I & II
NEVER LOVE AGAIN
THUG ADDICTION
By **Kim Kaye**
THE KING CARTEL I, II & III
By **Frank Gresham**
THESE NIGGAS AIN'T LOYAL I, II & III
By **Nikki Tee**
GANGSTA SHYT I II &III
By **CATO**
THE ULTIMATE BETRAYAL
By **Phoenix**
BOSS'N UP I & II
By **Royal Nicole**
I LOVE YOU TO DEATH

Ghost

By **Destiny J**
I RIDE FOR MY HITTA
I STILL RIDE FOR MY HITTA
By **Misty Holt**
LOVE & CHASIN' PAPER
By **Qay Crockett**
TO DIE IN VAIN
By **ASAD**

BOOKS BY LDP'S CEO, CA$H

TRUST IN NO MAN
TRUST IN NO MAN 2
TRUST IN NO MAN 3
BONDED BY BLOOD
SHORTY GOT A THUG
THUGS CRY
THUGS CRY 2
THUGS CRY 3
TRUST NO BITCH
TRUST NO BITCH 2
TRUST NO BITCH 3
TIL MY CASKET DROPS
RESTRAINING ORDER
RESTRAINING ORDER 2
IN LOVE WITH A CONVICT

Coming Soon

BONDED BY BLOOD 2
BOW DOWN TO MY GANGSTA

CPSIA information can be obtained
at www.ICGtesting.com
Printed in the USA
LVHW022335160220
647111LV00006B/59